TO WIELD A PLAGUE

PASSAGE TO DAWN: COMPANION

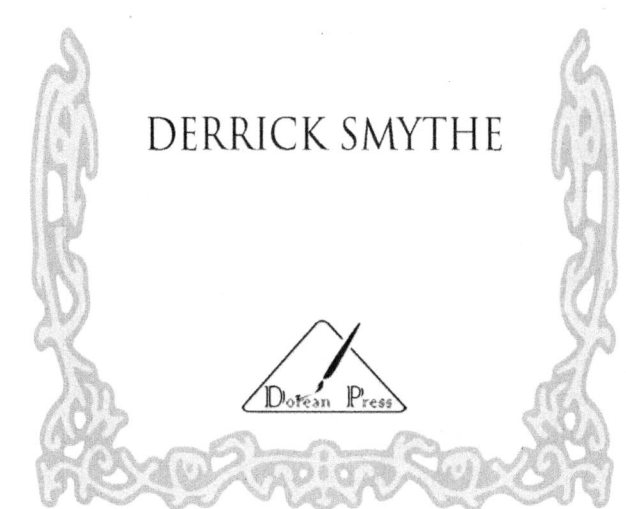

DERRICK SMYTHE

Dorean Press

Copyright

To Wield a Plague: A Passage to Dawn Companion
© 2022 Derrick Smythe, All Rights Reserved.
Published by Dorean Press, Cicero, New York

978-1-7340953-8-8 (paperback)
978-1-7340953-7-1 (eBook)

www.derricksmythe.com

This is a work of fiction. The events and persons are imagined. Any resemblance to actual events, or to persons, alive or dead, is purely coincidental.

Without limiting the rights under copyright reserved above, no part of this publication may be reproduced, stored in or introduced into a retrieval system, or transmitted in any form or by any means (electronic, mechanical , photocopying, recording or otherwise), without the prior written permission of both the copyright owner and the above publisher of this book, except by a reviewer who wishes to quote brief passages in connection with a review written for insertion in a magazine, newspaper, broadcast, website, blog or other outlet.

Editor: Carolyn Haley & Sarah Chorn
Cover Illustration: Ömer Burak Önal
Map Illustration: Derrick Smythe
Design: Derrick Smythe

Acknowledgments

One week prior to the publication of my debut novel, *The Other Magic*, I gave myself a belated birthday present: I told my family that I had written a book. Prior to this, knowledge of my secret decade-long project had been limited to a very small inner circle. My reasons for keeping it a secret were numerous, but no part of this decision had anything to do with a lack of perceived support. If anything, I suspected I would receive more well-meaning prodding and care than I would have wished at the time. Since learning about my not-so-little secret passion that doubles as my excuse for the occasional stints of reclusiveness, my parents, brothers, and extended family have been nothing but supportive. I am truly blessed.

To my readers, without whom this book would not have been possible, I pray your patience and support are repaid in kind with *To Wield a Plague* and many more!

To Podium Audio for transforming my stories into incredible audio content. Greg Patmore's narration breathes life into the characters and illuminates this world in ways I never thought possible.

To my local writing group, who continues to keep me on my toes, never afraid to dash the hope that I might ever write an infallible first draft.

To my most trusted beta readers, Davida, Bryan, Dan, and Ed, who provided critical feedback that allowed for To Wield a Plague to become the best book it could be.

To my editors, Carolyn and Sarah, for their transformative work on this story. I count myself lucky to work with two of the best in the industry.

To my biggest supporter, my wife, Kelly, who is not only my first-look editor, but can now add co-author to her résumé since she actually wrote a few scenes in this book. This began as a passive-aggressive means of proving she was right after a disagreement over some changes she had suggested. After reading what she wrote, I readily conceded. With her blessing, I have incorporated segments of her writing, which improved the story greatly.

And finally, to God, whose subtle nudges encouraged me to begin this journey in the first place, and who keeps me far from despair whenever things don't go according to my plan.

Author's Note

TO WIELD A PLAGUE IS a standalone adventure that can be enjoyed regardless of whether you've read *The Other Magic*, *The Other Way*, or Passage to Dawn companion stories such as *To Earn the Sash*.

This story chronicles one of my favorite characters, one I had otherwise been unable to explore further within the main books in the Passage to Dawn series. Thus, Dwapek has been given a story of his own. These events have specific relevance within the main series and may foreshadow happenings yet to occur within the series. If you are someone who enjoys literary Easter eggs, this story is especially for you.

The Northlands

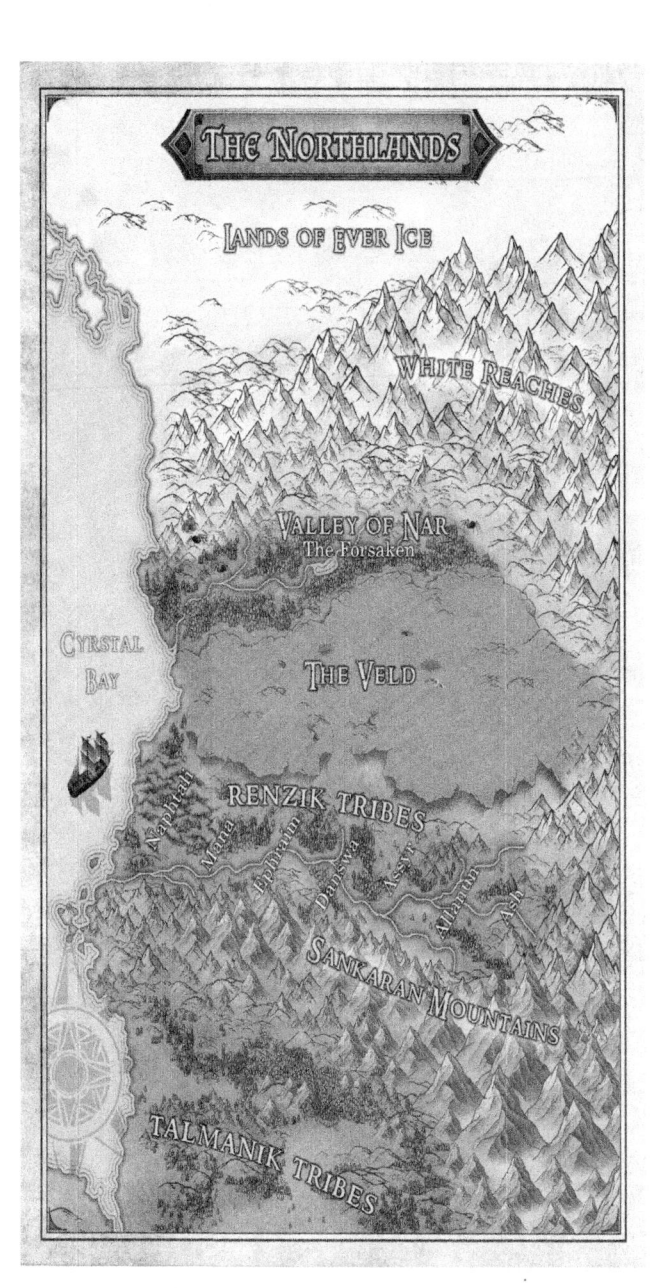

Lands of Ever Ice

White Reaches

Valley of Nar
The Forsaken

Cyrstal Bay

The Veld

Renzik Tribes

Naphtali · Mana · Ephraim · Danisma · Asyr · Atharim · Ash

Sankaran Mountains

Talmanik Tribes

TO
WIELD
A
PLAGUE

Chapter 1

"Think I should go for the eye or the heart?"

Dwapek's father, Aldrek, the Sachem of their tribe, remained silent as they trudged toward the Veld.

Excitement over his first hunt was too great to be cowed by the strong winds that caused the occasional word to go missing.

"Father! Father!"

Aldrek reluctantly looked Dwapek's way.

All right, he's listening. "Should I go for the eye or the heart? How about the throat?"

Sachem Aldrek's round, pronounced nose crinkled before he returned to face forward. "I think you should be preparing yourself for the silence of the Veld, should you succeed. This is not one of your frivolous sagas, this is reality. Do not fool with fancy." His father lengthened his stride and Dwapek fell behind, his zeal deflated.

His mother, Geothelis, reached over and patted his shoulder. "Don't worry about him. He'll change his tune once he sees how hard you've been working to improve. Just you wait."

Dwapek acknowledged his mother's comforting words with a nod, then slowed to avoid further conversation. He appreciated the sentiment, but his father was at least partially right: he needed to prepare. He would have to outthrow his father before he was even eligible to enter the Veld, let alone join the hunt. He should not be wasting time commiserating with his mother. He was here to prove his manhood.

Up ahead, Dwapek spotted a Renzik camp. He quickly counted seven caribou-skin tents, all in the domed style, which meant they likely belonged to a hunting party much like their own, only from Tribe Ash. Dwapek sighed in annoyance, for it would be considered rude to pass by without stopping to break bread with their kinsmen. Considering the lack of cookfire smoke, this would cost them half a day.

As they drew closer, Dwapek saw no movement. Had the entire party drunk themselves into a late-morning slumber? No sooner did Dwapek have this thought than his foot hit something hard in the tall grass. He tripped and fell to the side, cursing. The ordinarily soft, wavy grass leading up to the Veld felt more like brittle straw against his face. Rising to his feet, he attempted to locate the cause of his untimely fall.

He expected a small, downed tree, perhaps an unseen rock. Instead, he found a deerskin boot. *What's a boot doing out—*

He gasped as the grass stirred in the breeze, revealing the rest of the body. An unmoving body. The twisted expression of torment frozen upon the corpse's face told of great suffering. Dwapek was soon joined by five others, staring wide-eyed at the horrifying corpse. The wind picked up and Dwapek caught the stench of the death's rot. He turned away and gagged.

His father yelled, "Check for survivors."

As Dwapek turned to regard the rest of the camp, he noticed another discomforting oddity: the grass. It was brown and bent awkwardly in the wind. The crunching that accompanied each step confirmed what he had been thinking: it was all dead. Everything here was dead.

The others in the party fanned out, and Dwapek played his role. Reluctantly opening the flap of the nearest tent, he recoiled as a powerful stench of decay assailed him and he stumbled out coughing.

The entirety of the camp was gone. Dwapek saw the beads and headdress of a Shaman outfitting a corpse that seemed to have perished in the middle of crawling, perhaps in some vain attempt to escape whatever had befallen this place. The image was more disturbing than even the stench. How could an entire camp of people die like this? The grass, too?

"No flesh wounds," said his father. "We should not linger here. They have been cursed."

Shaman Varik nodded in agreement. "Dark magic. Let us say the words and be gone."

"We need to bury them!" shouted Theresak, her voice cracking with anger. "We can't just leave them for the—"

Shaman Varik cut her off. "We know not the cause of such affliction, but whatever it was, it took every last soul. The very soil beneath our boots has been damned! To handle these bodies could mean to share in their fate. Let us gather round, say the words, and be gone. We may have already done too much."

The group resumed their march toward the Veld. Dwapek's father finally asked Shaman Varik, "What offense could bring about such wrath?"

The Shaman shook his head. "I cannot imagine. Let us just pray we remain in the favor of the Earthmother and her children."

The party moved on in silence. Dwapek felt a heavy cloak of guilt weighing down each step, the burden of avoiding whatever misfortune had befallen the others. This was irrational and unjustified, he knew, but the feeling lingered nonetheless, tempering his ability to fully prepare himself for what was to come.

The boy finally found his strength, wiped tears shed for the fallen, and chided himself. *Feeling sorry will not bring a single one of them back. Father is right. I need to prepare my mind for the throw, as well as my silence.* As soon as they passed the ridge marking the beginning of the Veld, speech of any kind would be strictly prohibited until reaching the Valley of Nar. Violating this sacred law was punishable by tribal banishment. This, of course, seemed a triviality after what he'd just witnessed. Apparently the gods were taking a more active role in assuring vengeance of all kinds.

Not long after, the group of fifteen Renzik male and female hunters fanned out to form a line before a spire of weathered stone shaped to resemble a spear, though Dwapek had to use his imagination to see it. This stone was surrounded by brittle grass and a smattering of misshapen bushes and small trees. No other vegetation was stubborn enough to endeavor against the cold, windy steppe known as the Veld. The distant ridge marking the Veld was perhaps half a day's walk, a place of blessings and curses, monsters, and sustenance. They had arrived.

Dwapek stepped into the vacant space between the tribal Sachem and his mother. His nerves swirled in his stomach like winter flakes blown down from the north. In just a few days, he could—no, he *would*—return a full-fledged Renzik man, earning not only the respect of his tribe but perhaps also that of his father. He had been waiting for this day his entire life!

He stood in silent anticipation as Shaman Varik raised his staff and spoke. "The first stage in a Renzik's ascent to adulthood is the throw. As is tradition, the father of the Renzik in question will throw his spear in the direction of the Veld. If no such father lives, or is able, a sponsor will take this role. Who stands to throw on behalf of the eligible Renzik, Dwapek?"

Silence.

Dwapek dared not look over at his father, the Sachem.

Gods, why isn't he moving? He wouldn't let me come all this way only to deny me the right, would he? I'm of age!

Just as Dwapek gathered the courage to turn his head and question his father, the Sachem stepped forward and spoke loudly, if unenthusiastically. "I, Sachem Aldrek of Tribe Danswa, stand for Dwapek of Tribe Danswa."

His father's hesitation was further evidence to Dwapek of Aldrek's disdain. Intentional or not, the barb stung.

Shaman Varik resumed the ritual speech with stoic indifference. "The father will now step forward and throw his spear into the Veld with all his might." In truth, the father's spear was nearly always thrown with minimal effort to ensure the child wasn't barred from the hunt by something of mere symbolic value. However, Dwapek had no such illusions; he would have been a fool to believe that his father would make this easy for him. "The Renzik in question must then outthrow their father, a sign that the new generation has come to usher in renewal of body and mind to the tribe."

The thought transported Dwapek back to the roving merchant whose visit had finalized Aldrek's contempt toward his son. Dwapek vividly recalled his first and only encounter with visitors from the land of men to the south. Those humans had been twice and more the height of the tallest Renzik, though not nearly as thick.

Most Renziks had believed humans to be more legend than truth until they arrived in the village. Reading about them was one thing, but these were in the flesh. Tall, gangly merchants seeking trade like any other. As was customary among Dwapek's people, the guests had been invited to share a meal by the fire before any discussion of commerce was permitted. Dwapek and the other children had kept their distance while the adults broke bread. The following day, the wagons had been set up to display their wares.

Dwapek hid behind a tent with the other children, spying on the party of men, feeling very clever as he asked, "Why do men wear boots filled with rocks?"

The others looked around confusedly. A perpetually annoying girl named Fusa whined, "Humans do not wear rocks in their boots."

"Sure they do," replied Dwapek as he winked at the others. "Because if they didn't, they'd blow away in the wind!"

This had elicited the desired laughter, but as the chuckles died down, one remained: deeper, throatier than the rest. This was no child. Dwapek whirled to see who had invaded their private show. "Hey! What are you—"

Dwapek stared directly at the waist of a human. His blue eyes slowly drifted up to stare into the shadowy darkness behind the drawn cowl of the tallest two-legged figure he'd ever seen. From the darkness came a voice, calm, emotionless, and terrifying. "You know, there are those among us who would rival your kind with their stoutly shape. They require no stone in their shoes." He winked at Dwapek. "I, however, find that such shapeliness does not do well on the road, thus my companions remain wary of blowing away in the wind. Hah! I do enjoy a good jibe."

Dwapek was speechless. The man didn't appear offended, that was good.

Then Dwapek's mother, Geothelis, said, "Hey! What's going on over here? You younglings bothering our honored guest?"

The human released another hearty laugh, bowing slightly as the Sachem's wife approached. "Not at all. Not at all. In fact, I was venturing into the village to see if anyone was brave enough to try their might with the Blade of Taldronis."

All eyes widened in surprise, then shot to Geothelis, begging for permission to follow this man. Her expression hardened and the excitement in the air vanished. "We've no such bravery in our midst." Then she raised an eyebrow. "Do we?"

The stale silence hovered a moment before exploding with cheers from the children as they rushed to follow the thin man toward the wagons, Dwapek foremost among them.

Deleanor, a female Renzik with beautiful jade-green eyes, gripped Dwapek's coat as they went. "Can you believe it? The Blade of Taldronis!"

Everyone knew the stories, but that didn't stop an excited Deleanor from restating the legend. "The blade was a gift from the Earthmother after Sachem Faeldrek knelt before her on behalf of the seven tribes, marking the beginning of the covenant of the tribes."

Pendrik chimed in from the left, "The eight tribes."

She gave him a quizzical look.

"The Forsaken? Remember?" He said this as if she'd forgotten her own name.

She rolled her eyes. The Forsaken were one of the original eight tribes, banished from the land centuries ago. An irrelevant clarification.

"Anyway, they say every single stone in the temple of the gods was cut with the magic of the Blade of Taldronis. Few have been deemed worthy enough to wield it, as the magic only works for the pure of heart."

A crowd gathered at a massive, colorfully painted wagon drawn by an equally mammoth equine. To call the creature a horse would be liken to calling a human a Renzik. The difference in size was too extreme. The horses in these lands were hardly large enough to be ridden by Renzik children, while the creature pulling the wagon stood taller than this human's already towering form. How such things had been transported from the southern lands of men was as great a mystery to Dwapek as the question of the treasures concealed within the wagon itself.

The gathered children continued to chatter about the various myths surrounding the blade and Dwapek likewise returned to such thoughts. The blade was said to have had gone missing centuries ago, rumors and fakes emerging every now and again. All had proven false, and Dwapek had little hope that today would be any different, but the possibility was exciting, nonetheless.

Dwapek's eyes were drawn to a stack of leather-bound books among the man's wares. He wondered if they held stories from the land of men and, if so, what quests they might entail? What manner of monsters might they include? Of course, his father would sooner pay for dung than allow Dwapek to purchase more stories. Aldrek resented Dwapek's obsession with the few works his mother had brought to their family. He said reading made a man weak. Reading was for the keepers to keep.

The merchant flourished his hands and suddenly there appeared an onyx dagger with a golden hilt beset with white stones. The books may as well have disappeared. Gasps escaped the onlookers, followed by cheers.

The merchant asked them all, "Who among you believes themselves worthy of the Blade of Taldronis?"

The hand of every child shot up in an instant, along with those of several adult Renziks playing along.

A line formed as the man produced a stone the size of a skull and set it on a wooden stool for the test. The merchant hushed the onlookers with a gesture, then handed the blade to the first in line, Genevor, an especially plump female Renzik. She raised the blade over her head, eagerly preparing to plunge the inky-black weapon into the stone before her. "Whoa," warned the man. "Many aspiring heroes have sliced palms or worse in their zeal to cut the stone. Just press the energy of the world into the knife, and if you're worthy, the blade will sink into the stone with little effort."

Genevor slumped slightly, then she stabbed the blade into the stone—or, rather, *at* the stone. It bounced off with a loud twang, then fell from her hands as she yelped. She received only a slight nick, but it was enough to keep everyone else in check as they made their own attempts.

A disappointed Deleanor turned and pressed the hilt of the knife into Dwapek's hand. "If anyone is worthy, it's you." She smiled warmly before stepping away from the stone.

Warmed by the sentiment, Dwapek wanted nothing more than to prove her words true. According to the human, utilizing the blade required the wielder to push the magic of the world into the knife. This was something most Renziks could handle. It would be rarer that a Renzik be unable to wield at least some measure of the residual gift left over from creation.

Dwapek was suddenly nervous. No matter how much he doubted himself, he could not completely discard hope.

He drew power from within the earth beneath his feet. He had to reach deeper than normal after so many others had taxed the most immediate natural energy. Manipulating the Earthmother's power had always come easily to Dwapek, but as the son of a Sachem, excellence in every way was a foregone conclusion. Unfortunately, he was little more than ordinary. And being ordinary, for him, meant he was an utter disappointment to his father.

But still, the Blade of Taldronis . . . ordinary or not, he had to try. He pressed the power he'd drawn into the blade and felt the alloy drink it hungrily. Then he swung the knife slowly, not wishing to embarrass himself as some of the others had. He closed one eye and turned his head as if expecting some terrible fate to befall him upon his inevitable failure. Except . . . the knife continued right into the stone, stopping only at the hilt.

Those nearest him gasped in surprise and the human spoke loudly, drawing the attention of everyone else. "At long last, a wielder worthy of the blade!"

Dwapek recalled vividly the feeling of triumph, the effortlessness of the knife as it slid through stone with such ease it could have been cutting into water.

And then all came crashing down. Sachem Aldrek's voice cut the cheers to pieces in an instant. "What's this?"

After the situation was explained, Aldrek's attitude changed. "Ah, so there's hope for the boy after all." He held out a hand for the blade and Dwapek obliged. "If Dwapek is the only one to have succeeded, then our Shamans have done poorly with this generation."

Geothelis said, "Actually, several of our more skilled adults also—"

Aldrek spoke over her. "It's no wonder we struggle to remain relevant among the tribes."

Dwapek felt his father draw in power before stabbing at the large rock. It skidded and sparked harmlessly to the side, and Aldrek cursed. He dropped the knife, blood oozing from his open palm, then whirled on the human. "What game are you playing at, swindler?"

The hooded figure ignored Aldrek's question as he retrieved the tool. He finally said, "The magic of this blade perceives more than just current ability. It—"

"A parlor trick at the expense of my authority and my people! Take your wiles and be gone. Return to this land at your own peril, for it will mean your deaths."

Geothelis said, "But what of the Blade of Taldronis? Our son is able to—"

"The Blade of Taldronis is a myth. This blade is a ploy."

Still, the damage had been done. That Aldrek's son had surpassed him in his command of the Earthmother's gifts were the least of the rumors that spread in the following days. Dwapek even heard stories of "wielder adept." Apparently being more than ordinary was only acceptable so long as it didn't outmatch the skills of his father.

"Don't go around thinking you're something special. A cruel game is all that was. Probably paid to come here by Sachem Horgath or Sachem Taeldrek. Perhaps both. They'd love to see me ousted after opposing their plans to negotiate new borders. Petty and foolish to think such a trivial act would work. Only a fool would believe a child like you could outmatch the skills of a Sachem. My enemies grow desperate."

Shame overwhelmed Dwapek as he realized the role he'd played in his enemy's games, a cruel betrayal of the gods. "I'm sorry, Father."

Aldrek waved a hand. "Fetch your mother some water for dinner. I believe you are worthy of *that* task."

Dwapek had not seen another human, nor had he heard another kind word from his father, since.

He shook his head to clear it of the traumatizing memory. He needed positive thoughts. Waiting for the throw, Geothelis offered a warm, reassuring smile that calmed Dwapek's nerves and gave him the confidence that everything would go according to plan, that this hunt would be one of the best experiences of his life. She had asked her own brother to work with him on his throwing technique, and Dwapek had poured his heart and soul into the training that would prepare him for this very moment. A moment that would prove his worth as a Renzik.

Sachem Aldrek raised his spear.

So it begins . . .

<hr />

Dwapek's father stepped back, cocked his arm, and a tingle of summoned energy could be felt flowing forth from the earth. With a few short shuffles forward, Aldrek slammed his fur-covered boot into the ground and sent his spear spiraling into the northerly wind. It flew like a meteor, striking the distant knee-high grass with such force Dwapek almost thought he heard the thud. The wooden shaft flexed upon impact.

The onlookers gasped, as did Dwapek as he stared at the mark so far from where they stood. He realized his training had been all for naught. He could not hope to outdo this throw. He would soon be on his way back to the foothills and their village, unable to participate in the hunt, unable to attend tribal meetings, unable to even take a wife. Beautiful Deleanor, his "promised," would be so disappointed. He could picture her grief-stricken expression, or perhaps even anger, maybe betrayal. Surely she would turn her attention elsewhere once she realized she would have to wait at least another year, only for him to fail again.

Why? Why did his father hate him so? It couldn't all stem from the visit from the humans, could it? Perhaps he wasn't suited to rule the tribe as his father and grandfather had, but that didn't mean he couldn't contribute. His father's doubt hurt, but it also infuriated him. Who was Aldrek to decide when he was ready to be a man? Sachem or not, this was beyond the scope of his dominion. Well, according to tradition, it was not, but it wasn't supposed to happen like this. *It won't happen like this.*

Dwapek gritted his teeth and rolled his throwing shoulder to loosen the muscles. His tan deerskin coat was tied at the waist with a leather belt. His jacket and boots, worn, comfortable, and familiar, allowed unfettered movement while his wool underclothes kept his temperature perfectly regulated in such a cold, unforgiving climate. A leather jerkin and various matching patches added a layer of protection from the wide array of dangers that might lurk in the Veld and beyond.

Shaking out his nerves, he hefted his spear, and with the full fury of his rage pumping through his veins, he glared at the ridge that separated the southern foothills from the Veld. Then he whispered a prayer. "Earthmother, I beseech thee to borrow the power of thy world, for it is not mine to take but thine to give." Dwapek extended his mind into the world around him, reaching for the residual energy he would need to surpass his father's throw. There was enough strength in the grass to fill him, but it would resist his pull and he would waste much of his own energy just trying to extract it. He searched deeper, finding sod, but it was filled with living grubs, worms, and creatures unknown, which would also limit the efficiency of the power he drew. Then he felt what he was really looking for: hard stone just an arm's length beneath the grassy sod. He opened his mind fully to grip the energy hiding within, then drew it deeply. Dwapek pulled in as much as his young body could handle.

He shook, brimming with more power than he had ever held as he waited for the near constant northerly wind to ease its perpetual beating upon his face. Several moments passed in silence before the lull. The windless moment held, and Dwapek gave his spear grip one last readjustment, then he lunged forward, shouted, and threw. He imbued his throw with every fiber of effort, passion, magic, and rage he could muster. He put so much into his throw, he lost his footing and fell forward upon releasing the spear. He kept his head down as the bone-tipped object split the air.

Everything remained eerily still, including the wind. Dwapek stayed where he was, one knee sunk into the earth, the other leg extending behind him, hands gripping the weedy soil.

Dwapek heard the distant thunk, and thought he felt the vibration in his feet. He had closed his eyes, but with no audible reaction from the onlookers, he had to see. He had to know what had happened. He could not hope to have matched his father's throw, but had his attempt been so poor that no one dared even react? Were they concealing their laughter?

Dwapek lifted his chin slowly and peered into the Veld. His eyes widened. He heard his breath, felt it linger in his lungs. His heart beat like the drum of an army marching in step toward battle. It was the only sound in the world in that moment. Then reality came crashing down. A cacophony erupted all around.

It was as if seeing the spear somehow released sound itself back into the world. The wind whipped across his face and several oohs and ahs of excitement blanketed Dwapek.

The success of his throw was impossible to judge, as the spears were so close. In fact, from where he stood, the spears appeared side by side, equal.

Without a word, Dwapek stalked toward the spears. He needed to know. As he closed in on the truth, his father's eyes narrowed, and he marched past. Dwapek's stomach twisted. He had been expecting an instant answer to his fate. Delaying such a weighty response was just cruel. The gods were punishing him yet again.

His father stopped, standing directly beside the two spears. His posture remained tall and proud, giving nothing away. When Dwapek reached his side, together they stared at the two spears. His father looked over his shoulder at the line of others making their way toward them before returning his gaze to the spears. Dwapek's lighter spear mimicked his father's in every way, right up to its angled entry in the earth. Every way except the distance thrown. Now Dwapek could see that the expanse his spear had traveled was a difference of only a finger's width. But it was a finger's distance *farther!*

He had outthrown his father! He sank to his knees and held up fisted hands in triumph. Dwapek opened his eyes as the others reached them. He looked at his mother, tears of joy forming at the creases of her eyes. His gaze then shifted to take in the reaction of his father, who, of course, still provided none. He wouldn't meet Dwapek's eyes, but his shoulders sagged as if in disappointment; the pain of that was crushing.

Dwapek's heart sank. It was a victory, a major victory, but without the approval of the Sachem, of his own father, it didn't feel like one. Aldrek finally straightened and spoke above the ripping wind. "The hunt commences. All who have traveled here today may partake." He met Dwapek's eye, and there was a slight sparkle. "Son, I'm . . ." His lips pursed in what Dwapek thought could be the beginnings of the word *proud*, but then he said, "I'm pleased you have shown such dedication to . . . something."

Whether he said the word or not, Dwapek knew his father was at least a little bit proud. A weight lifted from Dwapek's shoulders as he followed Aldrek over the ridge and into the silence demanded by the Veld.

Chapter 2

The Veld was a mostly barren landscape dotted with occasional wildlife that mistakenly ventured south of the Valley of Nar. Because it was situated upon a vast plateau, extreme weather ripped through with the vengeance of the gods themselves. To be caught in the open during such an event was a thing best avoided unless the goal was an early entrance into the afterlife.

The land beyond the Veld was their true destination. The Valley of Nar was a place of abundant life and fertility, home to the life-sustaining game that supplemented the Renziks' trade in coastal fish to the east. This was also home to the Nazca, eight-legged nightmares very good at killing and very difficult to kill; hence why the Renzik settlements were within the foothills of the southern divide rather than within the comparably lush Valley itself. Not that the foothills fully protected them, but the Nazca were far less frequent there, for the journey across the Veld was just as perilous for Nazca as for Renziks. Every once in a while, a Renzik party would be fortunate enough to stumble upon a Nazca carcass in the Veld before it was swallowed by the ever-growing grasses of the region. Dwapek's own spear tip had been fashioned from the razor-sharp tooth of a Nazca, or so he had been told.

The silent trek into the heart of the Veld was cold, windy, and arduous, but after succeeding in the throw, Dwapek was so energized, he fancied he could climb the southern divide into the lands of their distant kin, the Talmaniks. Brown pillars jutted from the grassy range like the bones of dead giants as they continued northeast toward the Valley. Game and other great treasures lay just out of sight, or so Dwapek hoped. The plan was to reach the Valley before nightfall, then set up camp. The hunt would begin early the following morning.

Not even the weight of the seal coats he carried for shelter could burden Dwapek's spirits. And in the mandated silence, the only objection his father could offer was the occasional scowl. *No different than any other day.*

As dusk approached, the rocky bones of the plateau increased in size and frequency, and Dwapek caught sight of snowy peaks in the distance, beneath which lay their destination. By this point, Dwapek's vigor had dwindled, replaced by fatigue. His lower back ached and he longed for rest. He had fallen to the back of the group, about a dozen paces behind his mother who, he suspected, was only lagging back as a kindness to him, though she would never admit it.

The snowy peaks ahead disappeared from view behind an outcropping of stone that resembled fingers reaching from the ground, surrounded by dozens of other narrow crags and ravines, some of which likely led to the Valley below. They were getting *very* close!

Dwapek stopped and placed hands on his knees to catch his breath, and then determined to catch up with the group before reaching their destination. He closed his eyes and sucked in several deep, full breaths of crisp air.

He stood, opened his eyes . . . and froze. *No. That . . . can't . . . be.* He blinked, hoping that doing so would prove his sight false. Instead, it validated his fear. The ferocity and vicious nature of the Nazca often caused the other dangers of these lands to go understated.

Ten paces before him loomed a monstrous silvertip bear. The species was rare nowadays, having been hunted nearly to extinction. They generally avoided Renziks, but this one must have been desperate. Regardless of the reason, the creature was here, and it was enormous. Its haunches reached at least eighteen hands in height, completely eclipsing his mother's small stature. Her head wouldn't reach its shoulders, even if it stood on all fours. Worse yet, the tough grasses and wind masked the sound of the creature's approach. Dwapek was the only one aware of its presence.

He shed his pack without thought as the silvertip headed for his mother. It would be upon her at any moment. With spear already in hand, Dwapek took two steps and threw—except he had been so focused on the bear that he failed to see the small rock in his path. His foot planted upon the stone, wobbled, then slid to the side, causing his throw to veer left. It punched soundlessly into the grass just behind the bear.

He was out of options. To speak while in the Veld was to curse in the face of the gods. It would mean tribal banishment. And yet to remain silent was to condemn his mother to a violent death. It was her life or the wrath of the gods. *Mother Wind, forgive me.* As if in answer, a sudden gale whipped across his face, cold and untamed.

Dwapek yelled, "Mother! Behind you!" He scooped up the closest stone he could find and threw, but it was his mother's quick reaction that saved her life. She spun and ducked beneath a swipe from a massive paw. Then the stone struck the creature's shoulder and it turned its blocky head in search of the offender.

Dwapek stood alone with no weapon, staring into the enraged eyes of the silvertip bear. It appeared to understand the imbalance of power just as he did. The creature slowly turned its body, its eyes never leaving his own.

The bear seemed both angry and confused, hesitating at the ridiculousness of such an affront. Behind the bear, Dwapek watched as the hunting party fanned out beside his mother, weapons in hand, their attention drawn by Dwapek's scream.

Geothelis drew back her own spear to throw, and Dwapek grew hopeful, but Sachem Aldrek caught her by the wrist, then wrapped his other arm around her waist. She struggled in vain against his strength, but he shook his head. Still restraining his wife, he cast a warning glare at the rest of the party as if to say, *Dwapek has forsaken the gods, you'll join his fate should you help*. No one moved. Blood of the chief or no, Dwapek was no longer a member of their tribe.

Sachem Aldrek relaxed his grip on his wife slowly, carefully, keeping his eyes trained on her. As his hand released her wrist, she ducked to the right and pushed away. He grunted, then growled in protest, but did not speak as she drew back her spear once more.

A fissure opened within Dwapek's heart. He had brothers and sisters. He thought of the youngest, Aldora, only four summers. Her sweet smile cropped by strawberry hair. Her high-pitched giggle whenever someone patted her head. And Tamorik, who had just thrown his first spear last summer. *I can't condemn them to a life without their mother. I can't.*

He held up a hand, tears in his eyes, and shouted, "Don't, Mother. Don't!"

She froze, but did not lower her spear.

Dwapek continued, each word as painful as the claws and teeth he knew he would soon face. "I made my choice as an adult. For the others. Don't waste your life on me. Your *children* need you."

He met her gaze and saw the pleading and sorrow. She took one step toward him, but by then Sachem Aldrek was there comforting her with a hand on her shoulder. She recoiled then swatted him away. Her eyes streamed with tears, but the fight in her was gone. She knew Dwapek was right. He had shamed himself and the clan and had almost dragged his own mother into disgrace.

A guttural growl reverberated from the bear, drawing Dwapek's attention back to the immediate threat to his life. Angry eyes fixed upon him, and the long snout wrinkled to reveal several long sharp teeth. Dwapek slowly stepped backward. Noticing this, the bear reared up on its haunches and released a deafening bellow. The bear stood three, perhaps four times Dwapek's height. He was often naïve, but in this case he knew exactly what was about to happen: he was going to be mauled to death.

His mind jumped from one bad idea to the next. He had managed to successfully commune with the mind of a rabbit, once. *Maybe I could commune with...*

That was a fool's hope, and he knew it. A bear's mind would be too wild, too stubborn to tame, even for a trained Shaman. Dwapek couldn't tame a worm. He settled on another futile instinct instead. He ran.

Dwapek darted toward the nearest outcropping of stone to his left; it rose perhaps two dozen hands into the air at jagged angles. He scrambled shamelessly to the top of the rocks, all the while feeling the earth shake as the savage silvertip bounded toward him in angry pursuit.

He grappled with ever-crumbling stones as his moccasined feet slipped with every step until he reached the top of a small spike of stone. Glancing back, he saw his pursuer roar at the darkening sky before narrowing its eyes on its prey. This momentary break provided Dwapek the opportunity to confirm two things: the beast would have no difficulty scaling the stone, and death was inevitable.

Even so, the will to survive remained.

Beneath him was nothing but crisp air and a fall far enough he doubted he would survive without grievous injury. Dwapek wondered why his instincts had taken him here. *Poor instincts,* he supposed. Watching the bear ascend with such speed, Dwapek improvised a new strategy. *Whether the gods have forsaken me or not, I'd best ask their permission first.* "Gods of the cosmos, I ask thee to borrow the power of thy world, for it is not mine to use but thine to give." There was no use worrying about overtaxing his bones at this point. They would likely have teeth and claw marks all over them soon enough. He drew upon the stone around him, pulling in as much energy as he could wield, then leaped forward and punched, sending all of the summoned energy through his fist and into—nothing.

His fist struck air. Instead the massive, clawed paw of the bear swatted him out of the sky like a spring gnat. His vision blurred as his surroundings spun—or rather, he spun. Finally, his right shoulder crunched into the thick grass that covered the region below. Spots swam before his eyes and he groaned. He had landed just a pace from the hard stone and was temporarily thankful for the awesome strength of the bear. Still, his shoulder was on fire and he felt the bite of cold air as it ripped into the bloody claw marks left in Dwapek's right side.

He stood dazed, and wincing at the pain, then ran across the grassy steppe toward the next closest grouping of tall rocks. For a moment, he heard no pursuit. Dare he hope the bear had determined him not worth the effort? The vibrations of a lumbering giant answered him, and he knew he would not be so lucky. With lungs aflame, injuries throbbing, and the confidence that he would be overtaken in mere moments, Dwapek reached another monument of weathered stone. He clambered to the top once more.

Planting his feet and gritting his teeth, he released a bellow of pent-up frustration for everything that had gone wrong in his life, not just today, but for his entire existence. His father hated him, he was exiled from his home, he would never have a family with Deleanor, and perhaps worst of all, the gods themselves seemed to take pleasure in his misfortune. The ferocity of his scream surprised him, but of course, like everything else in his life, the stampeding bear remained undeterred. The gods did indeed hate him. It wasn't until the beast came to within a few strides of him that Dwapek determined how much he regretted the decision to stand firm and wait.

His gaze darted cautiously around for another way out. A fuzzy bee buzzed past his ear, peacefully floating to a nearby apple tree. There weren't many trees in this region to begin with so to suddenly see one was as if Earthmother herself was speaking to him! How had he missed it before? This was the path to salvation. If he could reach the outstretched branch and climb the rest of the way up, he might be able to escape. He couldn't imagine the massive bear climbing up a tree. Inhaling deeply, and inspired by sounds of pursuit, he took a few steps back then propelled forward with as much strength as he could.

Brisk air swirled around him as he drifted between pinnacles. He understood for just a moment the majesty of clouds as he soared above glistening green apples and waving grass below. Time paused. With a THUNK the grass danced above him and the sky circled his feet. Or rather, Dwapek spun midair as a result of the silvertip clawing at his other side. Pain flashed across his midsection and his head became a muddled mess as he tumbled to the ground in the shadow of the overextended bear.

This is the end. This must be what a caterpillar feels as it's squished between two rocks. I should have given Deleanor one last flower.

He pictured her deep emerald-green eyes, unique among the Renziks, along with her more customary flowing auburn hair. She deserved a proper goodbye.

Then his thoughts moved to his mother. Should have hugged her more.

Then, for the briefest moment, he felt the tingling sensation of magic. Or he thought he did, but he couldn't focus on it. He was too busy tumbling through the air with a bear's claw in his side on his way to being crushed to death. He and the bear slammed into the grassy earth, and Dwapek was surprised by the relative softness of the weight. He had expected to be squashed like an ant under a boot, its guts smeared along the rock. This was more like being pressed into the ground by the belly rolls of one of his fat uncles.

Then he realized why. It wasn't the softness of the bear's muscled chest atop him that prevented him from being flattened like a stomped grape. The tingling sensation was, at least in part, the feeling of falling as the ground below them fell away. He and the colossal creature tumbled through the air amid dirt, rocks, and sod. How far? He would find out as soon as his deafening cry was stopped by the impact with the bottom of whatever hole he was falling into. This was quite the improvement compared with being torn apart limb from limb by the bear's massive teeth and paws, or even being crushed to death.

Disoriented, he was surprised to land atop the behemoth. The impact still forced all the air out of his lungs and a sudden pain plagued him as he fought to breathe. This was not the sudden end he had expected. *Couldn't be easy, could it?* He would wind up suffering after all, gods be cursed. But before his panicking mind could continue with complaints, his lungs filled with the glorious-if-dank air of a sinkhole.

Dwapek lay still for a moment just appreciating the act of breathing, and the sense of not being flattened like a mushroom underfoot. His instincts quickly reminded him that he lay upon the hulking form of a predator that had already clawed him twice and chased him into this place with clear intentions of ending his sixteen-year run at life. He clambered off the thing and ran—straight into a stone wall.

He cursed and rubbed his forehead, but managed to remain upright. Visibility was limited, to say the least. With night fast approaching, it would only get worse. He turned to regard the monstrous bear—who, to his great surprise, did not rise to attack. Did the fall kill the predator? How could something so big and powerful fail to survive a little tumble? Had the Earthmother finally had mercy on him? Was he free?

Before he had time to sigh in relief, his eyes adjusted to the darkness and he observed the bear's outline. What little light remained danced upon the silver tints in its otherwise brown coat. He was grateful to note that it did not so much as stir. In fact . . . he tiptoed closer, then watched and listened more closely. He saw the slight rise and fall of its back. *Alive, then.*

The impact must have knocked it unconscious. Dwapek determined it best to vacate the premises before the bear woke, and before the fullness of the evening stole away with what little light remained. He would not want to be caught out in the Veld when the deadly cold of night descended, especially with a giant hole in his fur coat caked with blood from where the bear's claws had broken the skin. He tiptoed along the edge of the space, dragging his hand along the smooth, vertical stone wall. Dwapek continued to check on the predatory mound of flesh that would be sure to finish what it had started the moment it woke.

After circling the space, he found no obvious means of escape. Looking up, he guessed they had fallen at least five paces. He considered climbing, but having felt the smoothness of the stone, he was certain this was not feasible, especially in the dark.

He slumped to the floor, placing his elbows on his knees, face in his hands. *Good to know I'll be keeping the bear from starvation for a few more days.* He was pretty sure the bear would be no more able to climb out of here than he.

A growl from the beast startled Dwapek, who jumped in surprise then grimaced. *Silence and a general lack of movement would be the best course for me at the moment.* Another sound from the bear and this time Dwapek thought it resembled more of a groan. *Perhaps that's how they yawn? Never heard a silvertip yawn before.*

Another sound escaped the bear's throat and Dwapek reassessed. It hadn't yet moved. Against all common sense, Dwapek rose to his feet and inched along the wall toward the bear's massive head. He could hardly see, but he could tell the general orientation. His foot scuffed a stone and he sucked in a breath. *May as well have shouted my location.*

A snort came from the fist-size nostrils, followed by another moan. It almost sounded to Dwapek like the creature was injured. *I've nothing to lose, anyhow. Let's find out for sure.*

"Hey, um, bear?"

A puff of hot air shot from the nostrils, but there was no other movement.

"Is there a reason why you're not eating me right now?"

The bear growled, but it was weak, almost a purr, more dismissive than aggressive. Dwapek inched closer, toward the bear's head, leaving the comfort of the wall behind. *This is unwise.*

As he came to within a single pace of the skull-crushing maw, the bear's outline grew more distinct. *If this is some trick, I'm the fool who walked right into it.* More pained sounds from the creature, but nothing further. Dwapek whispered, "Why aren't you chewing on my spine?"

An angry puff of air ejected from the nostrils. Dwapek fell to his backside and scooched away before realizing the bear *still* hadn't moved a muscle, *couldn't* move a muscle. He breathed a sigh of relief.

Then again, a slow death due to starvation wasn't a great consolation. *Why does it always have to be between two poor choices?*

Crawling to the bear's people-eater, even closer than before, he took a position sitting cross-legged within an arm's reach of the creature. It did nothing. He recalled years ago when his cousin, Gaetrek, fell on his head and lost all movement of his limbs from the neck down. Their Shaman had managed to treat the injury, stating that something in the spine had merely needed mending. Could it be that the fall had caused this bear the same fate? It seemed the only explanation besides an elaborate ruse to convince Dwapek to make this the easiest meal this bear had ever had.

Another moan and Dwapek almost felt bad for the thing. Aside from the fact that it had recently attempted to shred him into strips of Renzik tenderloin, seeing a creature of such strength diminished to a state of helpless immobility was still sad. Dwapek decided to attempt touching the beast's mind, though he doubted he would be able. Considering his lack of other options, it couldn't hurt. Dwapek recalled Shaman Varik saying that any animal could be reached, it was just a matter of the animal's willingness to commune, their mental acuity, and one's ability to convey ideas the creature was capable of understanding.

He did his best to clear his mind, then extended his thoughts into his surroundings, feeling first for the latent accessible energy of the stone around him. Then he reached the energy of the bear, recognizable because of the push it exerted against his will. This was how Shaman Paeltrek had taught him to sense living things. Plants and animals both clung to their essence, though the latter much more than the former. Animals radiated an almost negative energy, holding to their essence with fervor. Once he sensed the bear's energy, he was able to wend his way toward its mind. He closed his corporeal eyes to focus on his ethereal senses. The vague "shape" of the bear took form, though it was not a physical manifestation, but more of a general swirling of the bear's energy. The tightly packed sphere of energy at the center of the storm was the bear's mind. That was where he would enter, if he could.

Emotions slipped out of the silvertip like light beneath a closed door, a palpable anger mixed with—melancholy? No, this secondary emotion was stronger, like a deep sorrow. It seemed this creature, bestial as it may be, understood the simple concept of its own mortality. There was no fear, just sorrow and anger. Feeling along the edges of this consciousness, Dwapek had no illusions about his ability to penetrate and control it. Even if he could enter, he was no mind bender like some of his brethren. Like most, he had failed to demonstrate the most rudimentary of skills necessary to be trained further in that discipline. Still, he pressed forward and in so doing, felt something completely unexpected.

What is that? This had *not* happened when training on the rabbit for his testing. This bear was aware of his presence, and not in the physical sense. There were no eyes to "see," but Dwapek somehow knew the bear's consciousness was staring at his own. And not just staring, but pushing. The bear was pushing him away. As it did, Dwapek continued to feel the leaking of its emotions, foremost among them now fear, but also desperation. Fear of him? That couldn't be. Fear of death? Whatever it was, Dwapek now had another reason to commune.

As frigid temperatures descended upon the Veld, Dwapek would fall victim to its effects. He experienced his first bout of the shivers and knew there was only one way he would live to see morning.

He stood and felt his way to the bear's stomach. "Hey there, Big Paw. This runs counter to all instincts on both our parts, but would you mind if I snuggled in?"

He paused. *Did I just give this thing a name?*

Dwapek did his best to press thoughts of calm and safety toward the bear, who continued to fight his mind's approach, though it did release a sad purring growl. "I'm going to take that as a yes."

When the warmth from lying against the bear proved insufficient, he squeezed into the armpit of a forelimb. Big Paw's only objection came in the form of throaty groans. Dwapek's chattering teeth removed any guilt he might have felt at utilizing the now helpless predator for warmth. After all, Dwapek wouldn't have been stuck in this sinkhole had the thing not been trying to kill him. In fact, had he not fought back and run, much of him would be on the other side of that fur, in digestible pieces. That fact removed all remaining qualms. It wasn't long after he stopped shivering that exhaustion overpowered the remaining irreconcilable discomfort that came with lying curled up with a creature that would just as soon eat him.

"Good night, Big Paw."

He slept.

The next time Dwapek opened his eyes, it was morning. His shoulder and sides stung as he wriggled his way out from beneath the bear's heavy, fur-covered limb. He felt his scabs cracking painfully with the movement, but there was nothing to be done about it at the moment. One could not mend one's own wounds. Not even a Shaman. He would be forced to endure until he could find water to clean them, hoping the rest took care of itself.

Using the much-improved light, Dwapek surveyed the hole he and the bear shared. It was an oblong circle about fifteen paces across. The walls of the de facto cell were mostly smooth, but now that he could see, he spotted several potential handholds.

Taking another look at Big Paw, Dwapek noted it was still breathing, but its eyes were closed. *Can't blame you there.*

Seeing the irregular position of the bear confirmed Dwapek's supposition that it had landed *very* wrong. He prayed that a good night's sleep hadn't somehow healed the thing. A deep rumble in his stomach reminded Dwapek it was time to get out of there. The longer he waited, the weaker he would become. Looking around, he spotted a fissure running almost the entire length of the wall with a tiny ledge leading to a series of other cracks from which to grip. This was his way out.

Dwapek walked over to grip the closest handhold but stopped when he heard a groan. He turned and saw the bear's glistening eyes watching him. He thought about what it might be like to have no use of his body whatsoever, then thought how much worse that might be if he was completely alone, left to die a slow death of starvation. How long could a bear last in such a state? A few days? A week?

A knot formed in the pit of his stomach, mixing with the acute pain in his shoulder and side as he began climbing. The physical and emotional discomforts intensified as he worked his way up. He stopped and looked back at Big Paw who, coincidentally, released another sad sound.

Dwapek shook his head and let out a groan of his own. *Do I really feel guilty about this?* He remained where he was, just a few handholds up the wall, then resumed his ascent, but his arms felt heavy, and his legs weak, and his injuries throbbed. Two handholds later, he stopped once more, conflicted. *Am I going to just leave the bear there to die? Yes, of course I am. That bear is the sole reason I'm in this predicament in the first place.*

Irrational or not, he felt guilt as palpable as the cold wind of the Veld pressing down on him like invisible hands. Looking at his freedom above, he wished nothing more than to continue climbing. However, he knew with certainty that he could not. Not yet. Not until this burden was lifted. Before he stopped to consider what he was doing, he had climbed back down and started toward the bear. *I don't even know how to heal it; don't even know if it can be healed.* He released a heavy sigh of resignation. Speaking to the gods as much as to himself he grumbled, "Fine, I'll give this a try, but if it doesn't work, I walk away guilt-free. And if this behemoth decides to eat me instead of thanking me, I reserve the right to curse you, free from damnation."

Of course he received no answer.

Let's be done with it. He placed his hands on the bear's thick fur, then, much like extending his mind into the surrounding world of stone and plants, he closed his eyes and explored the energy within. He wouldn't be able to draw from it like he might a plant, and it was far more difficult to sense each nuanced layer of organic material like one might do with something more static like a stone. However, with effort, he was able to conjure a visual representation of what he saw within his mind's eye. The areas hosting the most concentrated energy were the bones. *Okay, here they are. Now to find the spine.* He sent his mind along the skeleton, mapping the bear's inner composition. It didn't take long to find the spine, nor the area of affliction. There was a pocket of fluid pulsing with energy around two vertebrae. The bear's body was, no doubt, attempting to mend the wound.

He compared the knuckle-like bones of the spine before and after the injury but saw no fracture. *What's causing this swelling, then? Hmm, that would be a great question for a healer, wouldn't it?*

But then he noticed something. *There!* The two bones were slightly askew when compared with the gentle curve formed by the others. This, he suspected, was the culprit behind the bear's paralysis. *But how do I make them un-askew?* Dwapek had never done a healing like this. Closing an exterior flesh wound and mending a mild fracture were the most complex healings a young Renzik might be taught before adulthood. Moving bones around inside a body was a different matter entirely.

There might also be another malady altogether. *Maybe Big Paw struck its head too hard?* He doubted very much that he would be able to do anything about . . .

Focus. Focus on what you can do.

Dwapek sent his mind into the hard-packed stone all around him, drawing on the multitudes of residual energy left behind by the Earthmother. This brought about a rush of excitement, his body tingling with raw power ready to be released. *Careful now. Too much will leave your own bones brittle, susceptible to their own breakage.* The ever-present warning was valid.

Returning the fullness of his consciousness to the spine, Dwapek wrapped his will around the two pieces of bone. *I think this is all I need. Perhaps this is little different than healing a fractured bone. Just need to get you two to where you're supposed to be.*

He gripped both pieces of bone with tendrils of energy, envisioned precisely where the bones should move, then poured his magic into the bear. The bones resisted but he pressed on, channeling more, strengthening the intensity. Still, nothing happened. *Why are you not listening to me? Move!* He sharpened his focus and will further still. There was no indication that the bones might move and Dwapek gasped before falling to his knees, having forgotten to breathe properly during the struggle.

Reflecting as he gasped for air, Dwapek lamented; those two bones didn't need to go far, which, now that he thought about it, gave him pause. *If I press too hard, once they finally do move, they might very well go too far, exacerbating, not fixing the problem.* He recalled breaking off a dead tree branch to use as a play sword as a child. He had pushed and pulled with no result, then gathered momentum to try harder until finally falling on his face when the branch snapped. He had nearly fallen off the edge of a steep cliff as a result. *This isn't going to work*, he concluded.

Why he felt that he had to do anything was another question altogether, but the guilt in the pit of his stomach did not lie. *Fine. I'll attempt it one more time and then I'm out, guilt-free.*

If I can't move the bones themselves, maybe I can move the tissue around them. As he inspected the sinews of flesh and muscle, he spotted another irregularity. A thin cylindrical cord of energy ran the length of the spine all the way to the brain. What's more, this cord-like substance was clearly kinked and torn in the exact area where the spine was out of alignment. *This could be it.*

Further scrutinizing the damaged area confirmed that there was, indeed, a severe blockage. Dwapek surmised that the fluid gathering in this area was here because of the blockage rather than the positioning of the bones. How to fix this issue? He wasn't certain, but he was going to try. He sent as much raw energy as he dared, given how much he had already used, and willed the kinked cord to unravel. The result of this effort was underwhelming, but some of the frayed cords began to mend, revealing that the cord was made up of several smaller, distinct strings of tissue, all of which remained knotted. Supplementing his will with bits of energy from the earth below, Dwapek caused the threads of tissue to loosen enough that he could untie the cord before returning it to a single straight line. As the knot eased, he felt a flow of energy move through it, a trickle followed by a rush. The ligaments and muscles suddenly soaked up the excess energy to mend themselves, much like the process of a simple flesh wound. The bear's body knew what to do at this point, and now that it was no longer limited by its ordinarily small flows of energy, it did so.

The bear roared as the connection between its body and brain was restored, and Dwapek was thrown from his feet as the beast all but leaped to all fours. He yelped when the towering giant rounded on him, teeth bared. He suddenly realized just how stupid he had been to heal a being of utter destruction while trapped beside it with nowhere to run. *Let this be swift,* he prayed.

Big Paw shook its head from side to side, then shook its entire body like one of the wolves Dwapek's brethren had taken to turning into pets, shaking their coats to remove water after a heavy rain. The bear's muscles, fat, and fur rippled with the movement, emphasizing its massive size. Dwapek was once again face to face, utterly vulnerable, before a hungry savage silvertip who seemed to have little love for the two-legged creature standing before it.

He didn't dare move, not even as the beast began sniffing, the nose leaving wet slime wherever it went, including Dwapek's own burgeoning beard. It didn't appear to be an aggressive action, but he recognized the possibility that the bear was savoring the scent of its meal before consumption. His uncles had always done an exaggerated version of this during communal feasts, much to the chagrin of their spouses and the entertainment of younglings such as Dwapek.

Big Paw opened its monstrous mouth and Dwapek stiffened, resisting the urge to run, not that there was anywhere to go. The shiny teeth seemed to quiver like Dwapek's resolve, and the bear's warm breath was enough to make even the vilest Renzik gag.

Another roar escaped the bear's flesh-chewer, accompanied by a sprinkle of saliva. Dwapek held his breath against an attack as much as against the smell.

Then the creature snorted, turned away, and leaped toward the north-facing wall. Dwapek watched in awe as its long sharp claws dug into the hard-packed earth and stone. Instead of sliding back down as he expected, the bear continued up and out of the enormous hole. *Peppered pickles!* The size of the beast belied its agility, and Dwapek felt the fool for ever thinking he could outrun such a predator.

Big Paw peered down into the hole, expectantly. Dwapek walked to the wall where he'd seen handholds and shouted, "I can't just hop, skip, and bound my way out of this hole. You know that, right?"

The bear continued to stare at him. Dwapek hadn't the slightest clue what the creature wanted or expected of him. Their relationship was a bit . . . complicated, to say the least. They'd saved each other's lives, but the connection was tenuous. Despite this, he looked up and sent his mind toward Big Paw one last time, attempting to impress a sense of gratitude at having not been swallowed whole, though he didn't know if this was a concept the bear was capable of understanding.

Big Paw had recoiled at his touch the night before, but this time Dwapek felt none of the defensive pressure. He still felt tension, and uncertainty, but the resistance was no longer there. If anything, the bear was drawing him in. Dwapek relaxed and allowed his mind to flow into that of the bear's. He was suddenly bombarded with a barrage of images. They were disorienting at first, fast, blurry, and vague, but within a few moments they came into focus and he was able to sort out much of what he was seeing.

A scene played out before his eyes: several Renziks, a hunting party by the looks of it, then three smaller bears on the run. The vision cleared, replaced by the corpses of two bears, spears sticking out from them, and the third was clearly injured. He saw all this through Big Paw's eyes. The Renziks had fled upon her arrival, though one did not survive the encounter. The injured bear had disappeared over a ledge, and the next scene showed Big Paw's doomed search. The injured cub was nowhere to be found. The rushing water explained that. This mama bear had lost all three cubs, Dwapek realized. The animosity she felt toward Renziks was not solely bestial, or at all unfounded. The images died away, replaced by anger, sorrow, and confusion. The vision of another humanoid shape flashed past, this one taller, slenderer. A human? It held no weapon, but Big Paw seemed frightened by it nonetheless. Its features were obscured by a hood. Then that too disappeared. *What was that?*

Dwapek considered Big Paw's interest in his hunting party, his mother, and finally himself. His heart softened. This was no different than the cycle of retaliatory violence between offended Renzik clans and families, the original cause of strife lost to time. Had his act of mercy ended this cycle, at least between his people and this one silvertip? Perhaps.

Big Paw grunted, then turned away from the hole and disappeared.

"Good-bye, Big Paw. Or more accurately, Big Ma?" whispered Dwapek. The pragmatic side of him recognized that it would behoove him to be far away from the bear if and when she grew hungry and changed her mind about him.

His thoughts didn't linger on Big Paw for long. He was still stuck in a deep hole in the ground, in a place that would kill him with cold alone should he fail to get far enough away before the return of the night.

He needed to get out of here.

Chapter 3

Dwapek was not considered a particularly talented climber among his people, but scaling steep walls of rock was a common pastime for Renzik children of Tribe Danswa, who occupied the foothills of the Sankaram Mountains to the south. He quickly started up the wall and progressed steadily until reaching a point with no further handholds. He cursed. He had been confident while looking at this path from the ground, but it was now evident that no amount of reaching or contorting his body would bring this next handhold within reach.

Unless I can gather enough momentum and swing my body. His shoulder still screamed at him for putting it through such torment, but the alternative was death by cold. Gripping the highest point possible with his right hand, he swung his legs left, right, left, right, and left. Then he shot upward as high as he could, pulling up with his right hand while the momentum of his legs propelled him upward toward the handhold. His left hand extended and made contact with flat, solid stone still half an arm's length shy of the handhold. Then he fell backward toward the hard ground below. *My bones are going to shatter.*

※ ※ ※

He woke to a pounding headache among other ailments. The sun was directly overhead, bathing him in its warmth. It would have been a beautiful sight were it not for the fact that the stone walls framing this view doubled as a death sentence. Apparently *this* was the Earthmother's cruel judgment for breaking the covenant of silence within the Veld. He wasn't even worthy of a quick death by bear. The whole situation seemed unfair to him, but then again, who was he to question the will of the gods? He looked about the space for another way out, and to his delight he saw one.

At the far side of the sinkhole, two walls narrowed to a thin dead-end passage, creating a chimney. That he had missed this before was a testament to his current state of renzanity. He had been looking for handholds and tunnels so had failed to notice the much more obvious means of escape. Not that stemming the gap would be particularly easy. In fact, he wasn't certain he *could* do it, but it was the most hopeful he had been about anything since outthrowing his father the day before. The fact that he had no idea where an outcast from his clan would go once he was out was a riddle to be solved *after* his escape from this hole in the ground.

Stemming the two converging walls went without difficulty until the very top, where the gap widened to beyond what his short Renzik legs could reach. He rectified this by planting both feet on the far wall while his back pressed against the other. This worked until the top was just beyond reach. At this point, he was forced to turn himself around so that he stared down at the ground with outstretched hands pressing against the wall while his feet did so upon the other. He was high enough to be certain that to fall would be perilous. If the distance down was not enough, directly below him was a sharp, angry-looking stone. *Should have moved that before the climb!*

He inched his way higher and higher until, finally, his fingers felt the top of the wall—thick grass. He had done it! Except, his feet were still extended horizontally. Where the two sides came together was rounded and the angle made it too difficult for him to move, let alone shuffle to one side or the other. Dwapek saw only one option: release the pressure with his feet and hope his grip on the edge of the wall held firm.

His body was shaking with fatigue so great, his injuries felt like distant things. He didn't have the strength to contemplate his options further. If there was another way, a better way, he didn't have the time to discover it. He took three deep breaths, and then allowed the pressure outward with his legs to end. His body swung fast and hard toward the wall and he half shouted, half grunted as his chest struck stone. The thick, tough grass tore free, causing his body to go sideways, but somehow his right hand held. Trembling, Dwapek attempted to pull his now-vertical body up, but his single arm was far too weak. He cried out and swung his legs from left to right until his other hand was able to reestablish itself with the top of the wall. With both hands firmly gripping the edge, he found the last vestige of strength and heaved himself up. With his chest on flat ground and his legs still dangling over the edge, Dwapek wormed his way forward before finally rolling to his back.

He wept with joy.

Everything was numb after such an exertion of body and mind and he lay, dazed. He had no idea where he might go from here, but that would be a problem for future Dwapek to puzzle out. Current Dwapek was going to enjoy being alive for a few more moments.

He basked in this state for some time before coming to terms with the fact that if he didn't move soon, it would all have been in vain. He rose on shaky legs and trudged back to where he hoped his spear remained. He would then head north toward the Valley where he might find shelter from the worst of the Veld's elements. If the Earthmother was done punishing him, he'd also find food.

CHAPTER 4

DWAPEK'S LIPS WERE CRUSTY AND cracked, and the sky was dark by the time he reached water. But water meant he was no longer within the Veld. He had no idea where he was within the Valley aside from knowing he had cut a path through the tall grass at a more northerly angle from that taken by his clan—former clan.

If ever he saw them again, he would be considered an uninvited outsider, an enemy. To visit another tribe without the mark of envoy was a death sentence. No matter his mother's protestations, he had no doubt his father would see this law enforced should he encounter them within the Veld, the Valley, or back in their village.

Dwapek grunted as he lowered himself onto all fours. Then he put his face in the narrow stream and drank deeply. The water was icy cold, but his dry mouth and empty stomach invited it. However, Dwapek wondered if a quick death from the spear might be better than being taken by the elements or, worse yet, hunger.

The gods, with their ever-twisted humor, decided to answer this question for him. The clouds above parted just enough to reveal more than the contours of the small stream; they revealed a doe walking toward the water just ten paces away from where Dwapek knelt. *Elements take me*, he thought. *That is, if I can actually kill this thing.*

He had used his spear to ease his weak body to the ground so it was right beside him. All he needed to do was reposition himself to throw without spooking the creature. Thus far, she seemed either entirely aloof or indifferent.

Gripping the spear, he kept it low, twirling it so the point would face down when thrown. That done, he slowly extended his right leg until his boot touched the ground, sole down. He then pushed the rest of his body into a standing position. So far so goo—

The deer's ears perked up and its head swiveled, wide eyes locking on Dwapek, who had frozen in place. Too late. Dwapek drew in energy from the soil beneath his feet and sent a wave of calming emotions at the deer. His mind easily penetrated the deer's will and felt its desire to flee. He sent images of long wavy grass, and a speckling of trees for protection. Dwapek had never entered the mind of a deer, so he was surprised by how easy it was. He sensed none of the stubborn intelligence of a raccoon, or the mischievous, flighty inclinations of a fox. This deer's mind was more like that of a rabbit, fearful but easily tamed by a few thoughts of peace and calm.

Feeling guilty about manipulating the creature like this, Dwapek whispered a prayer to the Earthmother for the sacrifice of the deer. *It's my life or the deer's.* Then he drew back his spear and threw.

The shaft spun through the cold air, rotating beautifully, but Dwapek could already see it would be too high. *Nooo!* The deer sprang to life, spooked by Dwapek's sudden movement, and bounded across the stream.

The spear hit its shoulder. The blessed thing had jumped over something in its path just as the spear raced by. A near perfect shot!

As the creature continued to run, Dwapek realized that an emphasis on *near* was painfully appropriate. A perfect shot would have taken it down within a few strides. This deer, however, continued to run right into the thick brush on the other side of the creek. Dwapek cursed. Tired as he was, he needed to follow; if not to catch his kill, then to retrieve his spear.

Dwapek leaped over the creek after the deer . . . except, he didn't. He landed with one foot in the water, and sank to his knee in the mud. He growled and pulled it free, then barreled into the brush after his quarry.

He nearly fell onto his face as the brambles suddenly gave way to a clearing. And there, lying on the ground a dozen paces away, was the deer. This would have been a wondrous sight if not for the additional shapes: a half-circle of Renzik figures stood, spears and swords in hand. He was thinking now might be a good time to turn around and leave when a dizzying pain exploded in the back of his head and what little of the world he could see went sideways before disappearing completely.

Chapter 5

Cold washed over Dwapek's face and water streamed up his nose. He coughed, bringing to his attention the issue of his hands, which he couldn't use because they were bound behind his back. He was glad to find that he was not, in fact, drowning. There was, however, something painful around his ankles, which he discerned were also tied together. He squinted in confusion at the sight of three upside-down fires in the clearing surrounded by darkness. Looking further, he noted two thick vertical logs on either side intersecting to hold up a horizontal log as thick as a strong Renzik's bicep. A deer was positioned at the center, smeared with blood, completely gutted beneath the fire. *Idiot. Not beneath. Above.* They were both upside down, which seemed a bad omen.

Movement to his left caught his attention and he spotted the silhouette of a Renzik holding a bucket.

That explained the cold water that had roused him. Seeing this, he recognized a dozen or more similar shapes, some moving casually about, others sitting motionless around the flames of the three fires.

The shadowy figure holding the bucket spoke. "Good! You're awake. I was beginning to worry Faregood thumped you too hard."

That explained the throbbing pain in the back of his head, which unfortunately did not diminish from the increased pain caused by the blood rushing to his shoulder, as well as the deep cuts on his side.

He had a litany of questions, but he decided to begin with, "Who are you?"

The Renzik either didn't hear him or chose to ignore him. "You were hunting in the Valley without the blessing of the gods."

This was true, but these Renziks didn't have to know that. "I was separated from my tribe."

The Renzik seemed to consider this, then replied smartly, "If you had the blessing of the gods, you would not have been separated from your tribe." Dwapek understood the words, but they sounded strange, an accent with which Dwapek was unfamiliar.

Dwapek opened his mouth to respond, but between the unexpected accent and the content of the words, he was at a loss. *How does one argue with that kind of logic?*

"Your injuries are further evidence of the gods' rejection."

He felt mounting pressure in his skull, as well as throbbing from the injuries in his sides. *I'm going to pass out if I don't get cut down soon.* Unfortunately, he could think of nothing clever enough to convince his captor of this. He settled with, "Please, let me down."

"Tsk, tsk," said the Renzik. "You have violated the law of the gods. You have taken a life from within the Valley after the gods deemed you unworthy."

Dwapek was taken aback. "Unworthy? I wasn't . . ." How could he explain his separation from his clan? Would admitting that he broke the covenant of the gods make his case any stronger?

The man tsked again. "I need not know the details of your betrayal to know that you have lost favor. Your wounds alone speak of the Earthmother's judgment. One fact remains: the Valley of Nar is home to the Forsaken and the Forsaken alone. We tolerate small hunting parties traveling with the blessing of the gods. You are neither."

Cold wind ripped through Dwapek's body at the name *Forsaken*. Even in his current state, head ready to explode, he knew that name. The Forsaken were the ghosts of the Valley. Some said that they were the spirits of lost souls damned to reside within the Valley; others said they were the descendants of a lost tribe, one that had committed some great sin against the gods and were thrown out of the Renzik lands south of the Veld. In either case, he considered his current predicament worse than the hole from which he had just escaped.

The Forsaken man stepped into the light of the fire, his face now visible. His wide smile frightened Dwapek almost as much as the realization of who these people were. The man's teeth were brown and yellow, and several were missing.

"I see you recognize the name." He paused, then continued, "You're likely surprised to hear us embrace the name, since to your people this is a vulgarity." The man nodded to himself. "But we take pride in who we are and yes, you should be afraid."

Dwapek knew only two things for certain: these were bad people, and he was in grave danger. Make that three things: he was going to pass out.

His vision narrowed then faded. The man said something, but Dwapek didn't hear, or didn't understand. He blinked and then suddenly he was sitting upright, wrists and ankles still tied.

He was sitting at one of the fires, and because of the light he could now make out all the faces of those nearby. He counted seven in total, though there were more moving elsewhere within the camp.

Dwapek heard the same voice as before, and spotted the source: a Renzik man whose face bespoke danger. His eyes were black holes, though Dwapek recognized that this was largely because the man had rubbed soot around them. But he had one characteristic that was not cosmetic: four lines of raised scar tissue ran the length of his face, beginning above his right ear and down into the beard of his chin on the left. Based on the spacing, this had been the work of a bear—a big bear. His chest-length beard was a battle between red and silver, and he had deep age-creases along the outside of each eye where the black soot hadn't reached. His hairline, however, could have belonged to any youth. Dwapek guessed that he was seventy or eighty, middle aged for a Renzik who might ordinarily live midway through their second century. Then again, who could say how these Forsaken aged while living out here in the wilds of the Valley.

The Renzik had asked him a question. What had he said?

"Do you wish to live?" the man repeated.

Was he asking that because Dwapek had not responded to his initial question or had this been the question he'd asked in the first place? Dwapek decided that he needed to respond quickly no matter the case.

"Yes. Of course I do," he managed to say, ashamed of his squeaky voice.

The Forsaken's tone remained intense, a suggestion that he was still on the verge of murder. "Then listen very carefully, for your life depends on it."

Dwapek did his best to look like he was listening, which meant he bulged his eyes and leaned forward, nodding vigorously.

"First things first. You will tell us your story."

Dwapek waited for further details, but feared waiting too long so he asked, "W-what do you want to know?" His voice was still shaky and weak.

The man leaned forward and spoke in a low rumble. "Everything."

When Dwapek had finished telling these strangers everything he could, the assembled group rose in unison and moved far enough away that Dwapek could only discern mumbles. After a few minutes, they returned and retook their positions.

The man in charge removed his hood to reveal a Renzik face, though his beard was shorter than typical, more an extension of his chin than a thick length of flowing hair. He spoke less coolly than before. "My name is Petregof. It has been determined that you did not intentionally forsake the gods. The Earthmother and her kin are not so unreasonable as to condemn you for wishing to save your mother from certain death. And we now offer you a way back into Renzik society."

Dwapek was more confused than excited by the words. This was the Forsaken, a cruel people known for the evils they'd committed. Petregof's words sounded too good to be true, which meant they probably were. His father would never agree to allow him back into their tribe. Forsaken or not, these people had no authority over his father. Nor did they have any reason to help him. Either Petregof was lying, or there was a significant noose-shaped catch to his offer.

He continued, "You seem less enthusiastic than I would expect for one who has just been told that his life is to be returned."

Dwapek shrugged. "Forgive me, but I don't see how you intend to convince my father to agree to my return. Do you speak for the gods and Sachems now?"

Petregof chuckled. "I see." Then he smiled, the most genuine expression Dwapek had seen from him yet. "It seems I failed to explain the situation fully. You will earn status as a Renzik, but not within your former tribe. Based on what you have told us, you are correct to assume that your father would reject your return. However, our intention is to permit you to join the Forsaken."

Dwapek's jaw dropped. Joining the Forsaken was not exactly a return to Renzik society; they were outcasts, to put it kindly. To put it more accurately, they were damned by the gods—phantoms, hopeless, evil. Then again, fear of death was enough to keep Dwapek from saying any of this. Perhaps life with them wouldn't be so bad, though the idea of living in the Valley of Nar indefinitely was not something he imagined would be enjoyable, or long-lasting. He could always run away at first chance. He needed to agree to whatever was necessary to get his ropes cut.

Dwapek nodded and did his best to swallow the revulsion he felt at the thought of joining the Forsaken.

Petregof held up a finger. "Now, acceptance to the Forsaken is not so simple as a few words. You must first prove yourself worthy, for life in the Valley of Nar is, as you might guess, difficult."

Dwapek imagined himself attempting to do any number of things associated with the Forsaken: eating the flesh of a fellow Renzik, burning villages, or drowning babies. *I'm never going to be able to do this.*

Petregof continued to speak, drawing Dwapek's mind away from the imagined atrocities. "This case will be unique. If completed successfully, it will result in the Forsaken's return to acceptance within all Renzik tribes, though you will no longer be heir to a Sachem. I hope this would be acceptable to you."

If what Petregof said was true, this was as much as Dwapek could ever hope for: a miracle great enough to renew Dwapek's faith in the gods!

"I will do it." He knew he had just agreed to something about which he had few details, but considering the stakes, there was really no other choice. His stomach roiled as his mind returned to the problem at hand. He still had to "prove" himself.

"A wise choice. Though I suppose any fool would agree to such terms when their life hangs in the balance. The true question will be whether or not you deliver."

This did nothing to bolster Dwapek's confidence. "So what do I have to do?"

"You, dear Dwapek, are going to speak at the Naca Omin."

Dwapek heard the words, but they were nothing short of insanity. You didn't have to be the son of a

Sachem to know the trivial basics of Renzik government. The Naca Omin was an annual gathering of the seven tribes, during which the seven Sachems held a sacred, private meeting to discuss law, land, and trade. A Sachem might occasionally bring along a witness or expert to speak on one subject or another, but the guest would only be permitted to attend the part of the Naca Omin to which their speech was relevant. They would then return to their tribe.

Dwapek could do nothing to keep his eyes from widening, nor his mouth from emitting awkward laughter. "A member of the Forsaken would never be permitted to attend the meeting of the Naca Omin, let alone bring a guest."

Petregof nodded, obviously expecting this response. "Dwapek, I would like you to meet Sachem Freedek of Tribe Naphtali. Should you prove worthy, you will attend the Naca Omin at his behest."

Those words ended Dwapek's laughter. What was one of The Seven doing with the Forsaken, let alone a Sachem? Something *very* strange was going on. No—not strange. Strange would be seeing rain in winter; unusual, but not unheard of. The Sachem of the one of the seven Renzik tribes, here, sharing the warmth of a fire and breaking bread with the Forsaken, was unprecedented. Prior to seeing it with his own eyes, Dwapek would have said it was impossible.

One of those seated around the fire stood and stepped closer, the glow illuminating his round, bearded face. Freedek was similar in age to Dwapek's father, Aldrek. Looking at the man, Dwapek was confident that he had seen him visit his father once or twice. Freedek's long beard, braided down either side of his face the way young girls pigtailed their hair, was an unusual stylistic touch. This had garnered him the nickname Pig Face among his enemies.

"So you're it, huh?" Sachem Freedek said.

Dwapek looked from side to side, trying to determine for certain whether the question was addressed to him. He opened his mouth to respond with something along the lines of *Um . . . are you talking to me?* but before the words left his mouth, Sachem Freedek turned his head to face Petregof. "You've yet to prove the truth of this artifact. None of this happens without proof, and my patience wears thin, Forsaken."

Dwapek felt like he was going to be watching an argument over which he had no say. Not much different from back home with his mother and father, he supposed.

Freedek remained standing, facing Petregof expectantly. The leader of the Forsaken accepted the challenge, eyes glittering with amusement as he hollered, "Bring the vessel here."

Movement from behind resulted in the transfer of a small wooden box into Petregof's hands. Petregof set it upon his lap and sighed, rubbing the ornately carved wood. "Inside is an object of myth and legend. A vessel of power that may allow the Renzik people to inhabit the Valley of Nar permanently." Petregof gestured with a hand. "Please, have a seat."

Freedek stared at the box hungrily, eyes never leaving it as he sat beside Dwapek.

Dwapek too stared at the box in disbelief. The existence of such artifacts was fable. They belonged in stories; people didn't actually possess and wield them. At least, that's what Dwapek believed. According to legend, the Earthmother's children had used artifacts of great power in the Warring Gods Era, long before the formation of the eight tribes. Dwapek had read the Bone Caster Prophecies, which promised the return of such objects to the land of the Renziks to cleanse it of dangerous abominations such as the eight-legged Nazca. Could this man truly possess such a thing? If so, why share it with Freedek and the other Renziks? Why not simply use it to conquer? To conquer the tribes, seek revenge?

Petregof smiled. "My dear Sachem, the object in question lies within this very box. And yes, I will give you a demonstration of its power. But before this, I need to remind you that this offer is an act of faith. My people's status among our Renzik brethren will be restored."

Freedek nodded impatiently. "I applaud such selflessness. So admirable. Now the demonstration."

Petregof nodded. "It was not without great consideration that I have reached such a decision. I first consulted our bone caster, submitted the request to the gods, and they responded. The bones cracked and the story of our future was spoken. Reunification and peace. Everything thus far has gone accordingly, including the support of one of the eight. We merely needed our wielder." He gestured toward Freedek, then turned back to regard Dwapek. "Just days after setting camp, a deer stumbled into the circle, a spear protruding from its shoulder. Fate could not have been clearer. The boy's age and identity as the son of the Sachem confirms rumors about the existence of another wielder adept."

Wielder adept? That was a term used for only the rarest, most powerful Renzik Shamans. The only known wielder adept currently living had recently risen to the position of Sachem with the tribe of Ephraim. *Gods help me if Petregof believes me a wielder adept!*

Dwapek opened his mouth to deny this, but stopped as fears of what would happen to him when he did. Of course, if he proved unable to wield this object, he would be killed anyway, wouldn't he? *Shall I prolong the inevitable, or end my suffering now?*

Petregof stood abruptly and opened the small box. Both Dwapek and Freedek leaned in, expectant as Petregof withdrew a black pouch. He turned and set the wooden box down beside him, then loosened the pouch's drawstring and pulled out a fist-sized object, a sapphire of marbled blue and white. *Stunning*, Dwapek thought.

"Pretty stone," scoffed Freedek beside him. "But I will need to see more than this."

The leader of the Forsaken was unaffected by Freedek's skepticism. "What do you wish to see? What sort of demonstration would satisfy your curiosity?"

Freedek shrugged and opened his mouth to answer, but Petregof cut him off.

"I know just the thing."

"Oh?"

Petregof allowed a twisted grin to cross his face. "How would slaying a Nazca do for bolstering your confidence in this plan?"

Freedek squirmed in his seat. "I . . . suppose."

Dwapek was hardly surprised by Freedek's hesitancy. If the artifact wasn't what Petregof claimed, seeking a Nazca would be suicide.

"Excellent," replied Petregof. "We will depart at first light. We'll find a Nazca and I'll show you what this thing can do. Now let's get Dwapek to our Shaman for some healing, mending his jacket, and at least a few hours of sleep before the big hunt tomorrow."

⸻

War cries and shouts of alarm drew Dwapek away from the fitful sleep he had only just slipped into. He sprang to his feet, then cursed his fate. Petregof had insisted that Dwapek's wrists be tied together and his ankles bound to a tree. He'd at least been given a bedroll, but what did that matter if he was killed by whatever danger had stirred everyone into panic?

Petregof appeared beside him, knife glinting in the dawn's early light. Dwapek was thankful that it was the season of short nights. He shuffled back on his butt upon seeing Petregof's steel.

The Forsaken leader yelled, "Stop that. Do you wish to die?"

The man cut the rope tethering Dwapek to the tree then took his wrists and did the same.

"What's going on?" asked Dwapek.

Petregof cut through the rope quickly. "You're going to get to see the vessel at work a little sooner than anticipated."

"What? Why?"

Petregof pulled him in close. "Because the gods have seen fit to bring the hunt to us. Come, quickly now!"

A shrill cry rang out from the direction Petregof had gone. Dwapek was certain he should be heading anywhere else, but cursed and followed the leader of the Forsaken into the fray.

They broke through a line of small trees into a scene of pure horror. Ten Renziks stood in a half-circle with spears raised before a monster far worse than any of the stories could ever have prepared Dwapek to behold.

At the center of the formation of warriors was an eight-legged arachnid whose body alone could have been home to five Renzik adults. The long sinewy legs each ended in spear-like points capable of puncturing flesh as easily as a knife would do to meat. Upon seeing more Renziks, it released a piercing cry. Dwapek stooped to cover his ears against the horrifying sound.

Petregof stepped in front of Dwapek and shouted at his men, "Haldrek, where is Sachem Freedek?"

Haldrek replied without taking his eyes from the Nazca before him. "He ran that way!" and pointed toward the brush to the left.

"Retrieve him now," ordered Petregof. "He will wish to see this."

Haldrek stepped forward and struck out with his spear, then dodged out of the way as the Nazca slammed one of its dangerous appendages down where he had just stood. Haldrek shouted back, "I already sent Griffden after him."

"Very good," answered Petregof.

A moment later, a different Renzik holding a spear was not so lucky. The Nazca's talon-like leg shot toward the Renzik's boot, piercing hide and flesh. He growled in pain, then jabbed his spear toward the Nazca's neck. If he was aiming for a weak point, he surely missed, for his weapon glanced harmlessly off the shiny black carapace. What's more, Dwapek sensed a release of magic from that direction. Had the warrior attempted to imbue his attack with magic? No time to consider that, for Dwapek saw the full extent of the horror that was the Nazca. He had no idea if the hideous spider could see, but it turned its head to face its prey, revealing two shiny orbs above the mouth, above which rested two fangs the size of Dwapek's arms.

Can't get much worse than this.

As if hearing his words, the Nazca opened its mouth to reveal two rows of smaller, razor-sharp teeth, dripping with an oozing, black substance.

I stand corrected.

The Renzik, whose foot was still pinned, struck out at the giant spider once more but was again rebuffed by the creature's tough outer shell. Little puffs of magical residue peppered the air around the Nazca as the Renziks attacked.

Ignoring the others, the Nazca shot forward with open mouth and consumed the entire head and shoulders of the Renzik before it. The body of the headless Renzik remained upright for several heartbeats, blood spilling over the sides, before collapsing like a fallen tree.

Dwapek turned and retched, then wiped his mouth on his sleeve and forced himself to remain vigilant, fighting the instinct to run. The Nazca's spear-like legs had returned to striking out against its other adversaries working to keep it at bay.

He admired the poise of these Forsaken, holding their ground against the monster as if for sport, while others stood along the edge of the clearing to observe with much the same level of indifference. Dwapek had to remind himself that these weren't Renziks, not really, these were the Forsaken. Most of them had lived in these perilous lands for generations. The question of how the Forsaken survived was often explained by their practice of dark sorcery. Perhaps this was so.

Dwapek backed up to the edge of the clearing to watch the action. He recognized the frantic, frightened voice of Sachem Freedek to his right and, sure enough, the tribal chief emerged into the clearing, led by a burly Forsaken named Griffden; he all but dragged the Sachem along.

Griffden shook Freedek with both arms and scolded him as he attempted to turn away once more. "No!" He slapped the Sachem on the back of his head. "No! You. Watch."

Petregof spotted the Sachem and grinned wide. "Ah, Sachem Freedek, you've come to observe the power of the artifact!" Pulling the blue sapphire from a pocket, Petregof lifted it high.

He looked at Dwapek. *No, no, no, I'm not ready. I'll fail and we'll all die.*

Petregof's expression softened as if hearing Dwapek's thoughts. "You do not need to worry. I will give today's demonstration."

Relief and confusion washed over Dwapek like a sudden flurry of snow. *Does this mean Petregof is a wielder adept?* This would only postpone the inevitable revelation that Dwapek was merely an unlucky Renzik who happened to have stumbled into their camp. He was not some foretold wielder adept. However, this might give him enough time to figure out a way to escape before his failure got him killed.

Dwapek's musings over death were interrupted by the greatest coalescence of magic he had ever felt, far more than any single Renzik should be capable of safely wielding. Dwapek marveled at the volume of energy assembling in one space. So much channeled by one individual should turn his bones to ash a dozen times over. And yet Petregof stood tall and proud, the glowing orb in his hand, blue light illuminating the depths of dawn.

"This," he shouted, "is why the Naca Omin will grant the Forsaken their rightful place among their Renzik brethren! For with the power of this object, we will transform the land. We'll rid it of the Nazca and live in abundance, Forsaken and Renzik as one."

Then the blue light shot directly into the Nazca's chest. The monster screeched before black ichor exploded from a dozen places, one stream of it just missing Dwapek, who stood in awe.

The sudden end of the light as well as the vacuum of power that followed gave way to a moment stripped of sound, motion, and even time. Dwapek blinked in shock.

Then the momentary calm shattered, and the body of the Nazca fell to the ground with a crash, flecks of dust and bits of grass floating into the air to surround its corpse like a macabre halo.

Petregof lowered the blue stone of power and turned to regard Sachem Freedek. Griffden had released the man once the danger had passed, and Freedek showed no signs of running. He stared in wonder, mouth slack as he processed what he had just seen. Then he laughed. It started as a low rumble, but the intensity increased until it was bouncing off the trees around him.

Once he finally wrangled control of himself, he said, "You and I are going to change the world, my friend."

Petregof smiled back at him. "I know."

Chapter 6

A PROCESSION OF HUNDREDS, PERHAPS THOUSANDS, of Forsaken moved west along the edges of the Veld. How so many people survived in a land so cursed was a mystery to Dwapek, but he could not deny what he saw. For a nomadic people, they carried with them a significant number of belongings. Dwapek watched in awe as they pulled their full hupak'in sleds behind them, compelled to keep his own fatigue to himself.

"I still don't understand why you need *me* to present this artifact before the Naca Omin," grumbled Dwapek as he trudged beside Sachem Freedek and Petregof. They had been marching west along a narrow meandering river all morning on their way to meet up with members of Freedek's tribe. They would take custody of Dwapek until the Naca Omin.

Petregof raised an eyebrow. "Do you wish to become irrelevant so soon into your renewed life? Do you know what we do with things we no longer need?"

Dwapek shook his head. "That's not what I meant. It's just . . ."

Petregof added a response in typical Renzik fashion. "When a pebble drops into the water, it sinks just like a stone."

Dwapek harrumphed. "Sounds like something my father would say." The thought soured his mood further. Guest or not, his father would surely not react well to Dwapek's presence at the Naca Omin. "I just worry my being there may harm your chances of convincing the Sachems to restore the status of the Forsaken. Plus, they'll want a demonstration. Sachem Freedek's word alone will not be enough to convince someone like my father, especially if this Sachem has been consorting with the likes of the Forsaken, no offense."

Petregof shot him a wily smile. "None taken. I know what I am, and what you 'cultured' Renziks think of us. That's why you're perfect. Besides the fact that you are a wielder adept, you've also only been with us for a short time. The perceived taint of my people and these lands will ease, especially if you're the honored guest of a Sachem. Your father may not *see* you, but the others will. Sachem Freedek agrees on this point, and thus you *will* go. However, you're right about one thing. They'll want a demonstration. Before I send you into that den of wolves, we need to make certain that you're the wielder adept we need, yes?"

Dwapek stopped walking. "Huh?"

Petregof stopped as well, then patted Dwapek on the shoulder. "You're going to show the Sachems the power of this vessel."

Dwapek's eyes widened despite the midday sun.

"Oh, stop that," scolded Petregof. "You've nothing to worry over. If you're a wielder adept, you'll have no difficulty with the stone. And if not, I promise you a quick death. A win in either case."

"A quick death? That's a win?" asked an incredulous Dwapek.

"Better than the slow death we give to most who trespass alone in our lands." He patted Dwapek on the shoulder again. "Do not fear. You'll have a try as soon as we make camp. By tonight you will either know you are suited to wield the stone, or your body will feed the worms while your soul plays with the gods."

Dwapek gulped, but nodded as he continued walking. Everything about this entire situation smelled wrong, but what could he say? He was at the mercy of the Forsaken, and the same would be true when he was handed over to Freedek and the Naphtali tribe. After the events of the past few days, Dwapek remained hesitant to stoke any flames of optimism for fear they might blind him to the reality that his life was still far from restored.

He did have one additional question about the events he'd witnessed earlier. Well, several, actually, but he decided on one for now.

"Petregof?"

"Hmm?"

"I sensed small expenditures of magic during the battle with the Nazca, magic used by multiple Renziks."

Petregof scoffed. "I highly doubt that. I told you, the power of the vessel is—"

"No, not that part. I mean while they held the Nazca at bay. Each time they attacked with their spears, I sensed a flow of magic, yet even this appeared to do little damage to the Nazca."

"Oh, *that*." He let out a breath filled with mirth. "Believe it or not, you were sensing the magic of the Nazca."

The Nazca? Magic? Dwapek had never heard anything about the Nazca having magic.

Petregof chuckled softly. "I often forget how sheltered you Renziks in the south really are. Yes, of course the Nazca use magic. Only small amounts at a time. They do so to reinforce their exoskeleton, and they are quite adept. I believe it is no less instinctual than anything else they do. Their entire exterior ripples with small bits of magic. If you watch closely and have an aptitude for sensing the currents, you would see the exterior of the Nazca ebb and flow with it. I've never seen them do anything else with this power, but it certainly makes them more difficult to kill through conventional means unless you catch them by surprise."

Dwapek shook his head in awe. *And we're going to kill them all?* Power of the stone aside, it seemed like an impossible task.

"Petregof, excuse my doubts here, but what is the plan in dealing with the Nazca? Assuming everything goes well at the Naca Omin, and the tribes reinstate the status of the Forsaken, what then? Will you do the honors of hunting down all of the Nazca? There is only a single vessel. Is someone going to go out ahead and exterminate them all, then return with news that the Valley is safe? This whole plan remains quite fantastical."

Petregof nodded. "A reasonable question. I defer once again to the ignorance of your people. We, the Forsaken, have lived among the Nazca for centuries, and in that time we have made many observations about them. In fact, we've attempted, albeit unsuccessfully, to eradicate their kind. It is believed that the Nazca are all part of the same hive, so to speak. Like ants, they have a single permanent dwelling, and a single queen. If one were to enter their home and kill the queen, it is believed the rest would soon perish."

After having seen the destructive nature of a single Nazca, the idea of entering a place that was a home to more than one seemed suicidal, powerful stone or not. Dwapek had wisdom enough not to voice this opinion. "I see."

Petregof continued. "Now, something you should be aware of before touching the stone. It has other properties besides those which will be utilized to kill Nazca. It intensifies one's sensitivity to magic."

"Meaning?"

"Meaning, you'll be able to sense the use of magic to a greater degree while holding on to it. Someone wielding even a small amount of magic could be detected from a great distance. It's nothing to be concerned about, but if you're not prepared, it can take some getting used to."

"Well, thank you for the forewarning."

If his father had been right about any of his advice, it was the adage that life was best taken one day at a time.

⋖⋖⋖

Dwapek stared at the emptiness before him in a state of pure wonder. *I am a wielder adept.* They were the rarest of talents, gifted wielders capable of manipulating the flow of energy in ways most Shamans were unable. Dwapek had simply never been given the opportunity to stretch his limits. How many other adepts might exist, their abilities latent, never to realize their true talent?

I did . . . that? thought Dwapek. He had been all but certain that by this time today, he'd have an ax heading straight for his neck. Instead, an entire megala tree had not only been destroyed, it had been destroyed down to the root. A crater filled with loose soil and stones was all that remained.

Petregof clapped his hands. "Very good! Very good, indeed!"

Sachem Freedek and a contingent of his tribesfolk stared wide-eyed at what Dwapek had just done with the stone.

Dwapek placed the artifact back into Petregof's outstretched palm, his arms shaky. Petregof nodded. "You will leave at first light with the Naphtali. The Naca Omin will take place in seven days, and if all goes as it should, you will be one of us when all this is settled. Isn't that right, Sachem Freedek?"

The Sachem nodded. "Yes. Yes, of course."

Dwapek's face must have made clear his concerns, for Petregof's ordinarily cold expression softened. "Don't you worry. You did fine. And if you do as you've just done in front of the Naca Omin, you will not only regain your life, but you will change the Renzik landscape forever."

Dwapek was led to a small single-person tent where he was, for the first time since his capture, allowed to enter without being restrained. "No ropes?" he asked, more out of curiosity than any desire to have his ankles and wrists bound.

The Forsaken closest to him shrugged. "Boss says you are now a trusted ally. Now that you know what you might have at the end of this, you'd be a fool to run.

Plus, the entire camp perimeter is closely watched. So, no ropes. Unless you'd prefer it?"

Dwapek shook his head.

The escort chuckled. "I thought not." Then he became serious. "Better not foul up."

The Forsaken turned and shuffled away.

Dwapek didn't respond. *I'll try not to?*

He lay upon hard ground and curled into as tight a ball as he could, thankful for the windbreak of the tent. They were camped along the southernmost edge of the Valley of Nar in preparation to traverse the Veld to attend the Naca Omin. The chill leaking in the Valley from the Veld bit at Dwapek, whose clothes alone were not enough to keep him wholly warm.

Exhausted as he was from the activities of the past few days, his mind still refused to rest. Something was off. Wielding the artifact had been easy. Too easy. It had felt no different than anything else he'd ever done with magic, though that could be part of what it was to be a wielder adept. How would he know? Still, the stone had allowed him to channel power the likes of which he could hardly fathom, enough that his bones should have been completely drained of their matter, or dissolved altogether. This practice of using gems to help offset the effects of bone degradation was nothing new to the Renzik people, especially Shamans. It was well known that any object denser than one's bones would allow a wielder to channel magic through it first; or at least most of the channeling would come through the object first. This would work as long as the object was in direct contact with the wielder's skin. Only after the residual energy of the object was sapped would the bones be put to work in full. There were still limitations on how much even their greatest Shamans could wield, no matter the number of gems or stones, but these things significantly enhanced that volume.

So far as Dwapek understood, this artifact had far surpassed the capabilities of an object its size. Yet he had been there, and the results of using this artifact were undeniable. He had felt the explosion of power all around him as he drained the megala tree of its essence. Dwapek's confusion rested in the fact that he didn't feel like *he* had personally wielded much more energy than normal. Of course, that was the point of the stone, wasn't it? Perhaps it multiplied the effect of the energy channeled by the user and the stone somehow sent energy parallel to whatever was channeled by the individual wielder. However it functioned, Dwapek could not deny its effectiveness. Petregof's warning about its effects on one's ability to sense other magic was certainly no exaggeration. While in possession of the stone, he had become instantly aware of the slightest flows of power and was confident he could track the location of such an expenditure with precision. This quality alone made the stone valuable.

The fact that Petregof was giving Dwapek custody of such a powerful tool was another baffling situation altogether.

Sachem Freedek seemed equally trepidatious about the matter, and Dwapek could not blame him. The Sachem was about to take guardianship over a young Renzik about whom he knew very little. If Dwapek decided to turn against the Naphtali tribe, how many tribesfolk might he vanquish before he could be stopped? There was no telling, but Dwapek suspected that Sachem Freedek was pondering this very question and praying he wouldn't have to find out.

And Dwapek had his own concerns. He was supposed to attend a Naca Omin, present the power of this artifact, and then return to Petregof. But what if the Sachems decided they couldn't trust the Forsaken with such a weapon, even if the Forsaken promised peace and unity? Perhaps they wouldn't directly confront Dwapek while he possessed the stone, but an arrow to the back would be simple enough. And Petregof was sending him to the Naphtali with ten Forsaken escorts as guards. Would that be enough if Sachem Freedek decided he wished to take custody of the artifact?

Dwapek considered using it to try to kill Petregof, Sachem Freedek, and as many others as he could before escaping. However, captive or not, Dwapek was no murderer. Nor would this improve his situation if he did escape. Even with an artifact of immense power, he would still be all alone, an outcast in a desolate land. No, his best hope was to trust and pray this grand plan of Petregof's actually worked.

TO WIELD A PLAGUE

The following morning, before Dwapek was set to depart with his escort of ten Forsaken and Sachem Freedek's own small contingent of Naphtali, Petregof called him to his tent. Dwapek pushed past the animal-hide flap into the most lavish living quarters Dwapek had ever seen. This was a mobile tent, assembled and disassembled as often as the weather changed moods. Despite that, he was amazed by the luxury. That explained the number of carts and horses he'd spotted at the periphery of the camp as they entered.

He stepped onto a plush purple rug with intricate designs etched in gold. The walls of the tent were adorned in various colored banners, the origins of which Dwapek could only fathom, as they were not of Renzik make. There were chests, some open, some closed, but from what Dwapek could see, they were filled with riches of all manner: coins, gold chalices, jewelry, and gemstones. Others were filled with clothing, all dyed garments worth a fortune. Should the Forsaken be accepted as one of the seven Renzik tribes, their wealth might surprise the others. The circular oak desk was at least two paces in diameter, and upon it rested two golden lamps, stacks of parchment, and even a few leather-bound books.

"Impressive, is it not?"

Dwapek nodded, speechless.

Petregof walked over to his desk and placed his hands upon a small wooden chest. It was dark, nearly black, with white symbols and scrollwork marking the surface. Dwapek felt a small tingle of magic, then heard a click. The box opened, and Petregof reached in and pulled out a necklace.

Holding it up, he said, "Dwapek, this is for you to wear to the Naca Omin."

Dwapek stared at a chain of completely black metal links, adorned by off-white bones, each inset with a blue sapphire. He stepped forward to take a closer look, reaching out his hands as Petregof handed it over. It was indeed crafted of bone, though from what animal Dwapek could only imagine. Each was unique in shape, gnarled like a twisted root.

"I . . . what is this?"

Petregof shrugged. "It is a talisman of protection from injury during the wielding of otherwise dangerous amounts of magic. Now, I know the artifact can be used to great effect without such precautions, but who's to say what kind of demonstration those of the Naca Omin might require of you? With this you'll be able to do whatever is necessary without concern for your well-being. You will only have one opportunity to present the artifact, and it would not look so good if you went and died after wielding it now, would it?"

"Uh—I suppose not. Um, thank you," said Dwapek.

Petregof nodded and Dwapek turned to leave, lifting the necklace to place around his neck. "Wait," Petregof said.

Dwapek stopped and turned to face the leader of the Forsaken once more.

"You would be wise to keep the necklace hidden from sight. It is an item of immense value, and it would be a shame if someone recognized it for what it is and took it from you before your performance. If I were you, I'd wait to put it on until just before the Naca Omin. And be sure to keep it from touching your skin until you intend to use it, for it takes months to replenish its usefulness. If you channel magic before you intend, while wearing it, you will be without protection when you truly need it."

Dwapek slipped the strange necklace into the pouch sewn inside his coat designed to carry small tools, knives, or, in this case, a magical chain of bones. The added protection did little to dampen his concerns about presenting before the Naca Omin, chiefly his father. But it did comfort him that if he was going to die, it might not be from using an artifact of great power that he had only used once.

Chapter 7

Dwapek stared at the annual gathering of nearly every Renzik in the land. Dwapek, the ten Forsaken escorts, and Sachem Freedek's own small contingent seemed to relax as they left the Veld behind, giving way to a rise of land punctuated by crevasses and ridges that provided necessary protection from the weather and creatures that roamed the Valley and the Veld. This narrow strip of habitable land bordered the snowcapped peaks to the south, the boundary between the land of the Renziks, their cousins the Talmaniks, and the world of humans beyond. To the west was a great sea of cold, salty water from which an occasional seafaring vessel attempted to secure trade, or refuge from a storm. Renziks rarely permitted either.

It seemed fitting that it was the Naphtali tribe's turn to host the Naca Omin, given Sachem Freedek's role in the unusual upcoming proceedings. Tents had been erected as far as Dwapek could see, but his contingent continued past them, into the gorge where the permanent settlement of the host tribe had been constructed. The area between the Veld and the mountains was widest here by the coast: perhaps three hundred paces across, with hundreds of splintering passes to other smaller ridges, some natural, some carved over the centuries by the Naphtali. Each wall was lined with dwellings cut directly into the stone, and the past few generations had even seen the construction of several new tunnels and deeper caverns, though the Naca Omin would adhere to the traditional Renzik meeting place, the tent of the mammoth. All seven of the Sachems, and any honored guests, would enter into deliberations within a tent constructed of a single hide, from a single mammoth, supported only by the bones of this same slain creature. There were other temporary structures built for trade, especially during the weeks leading up to the Naca Omin, when thousands of Renziks would all inhabit the region.

Sachem Freedek led the group down a series of switchbacks toward the main crevasse, taking them past the tent of the mammoth where in just one day Dwapek would stand before the seven Sachems, his fate—and that of all the tribes—in his hands. The thought forced a shudder as Freedek led them into a narrow passageway.

Dwapek could see the awe and wonder in the eyes of the Forsaken who had been sent to ensure the wishes of their leader were carried out. While the lands beyond the Veld were comparatively lush with vegetation and game, they were also perilous; and those who lived there were forced to remain nomadic, more so than some of the eastern tribes like Dwapek's own, or rather the tribe to which Dwapek *used* to belong. He was now at the mercy of Sachem Freedek and, after this, Petregof.

Sachem Freedek stopped at the entrance to a tunnel and waited for everyone to catch up. "We're going to be entering the underground, and I'm afraid you will not be permitted to take any weapons with you."

The Forsaken looked about, attempting to take the measure of the others and whether they would comply. Sachem Freedek nodded and smiled. "No need to worry, they'll be kept safe and returned to you the moment you depart from this place. But considering the image most of my brethren have of the Forsaken, it has been decided that this will be the safest place for you. I would hate to see any unnecessary harm befall my honored guests."

Hesitantly, each member of the party disarmed, handing their spears and knives over to Sachem Freedek's men. Sachem Freedek spoke up again. "I apologize, but you'll all need to be searched, just in case."

Similar hesitant reactions gave way to reluctant compliance, and each member of his party was searched. Not surprisingly, several smaller knives were confiscated.

Dwapek's heart raced as the Renzik searching the folds of his parka stopped at the pouch holding the necklace. He pulled it out, stared at it. Worrying that he would call the attention of Sachem Freedek, Dwapek said, "It's a priceless family heirloom."

The Renzik continued to glare at it, then finally shrugged and returned it to the pouch. Dwapek let out a quiet sigh of relief. Something as simple as a common theft would have been enough to undo him. Not that his chances of success relied wholly on the protection provided by the talisman, but it would give him more confidence after what Petregof had said.

Sachem Freedek announced, "Let's move. Time to get settled in before tomorrow's big event."

They were led through a labyrinth of tunnels, far more than Dwapek realized existed in the home of the Naphtali. He saw more than just the light of a single lamp up ahead and hoped it meant the end of their journey. He had sensed the gradual downward angle for some time and grew more uneasy with every step. He imagined the weight of a mountain above and had visions of stone collapsing upon him. *And knowing the whims of the gods lately, I wouldn't die quickly. I'd be trapped in a pocket of air with broken legs to suffer.*

Dwapek trailed the others so he was the last to step into the circular room large enough to easily hold Sachem Freedek, the ten Forsaken escorts, and the contingent of armed guards. Dwapek noticed the uneasy posture of the Forsaken and thought perhaps they were feeling similarly troubled about being so far below the surface. But then he saw the raised weapons of the guards, and the outer ring of small rooms, most of which were empty, though a few appeared occupied.

Except these weren't guest rooms, they were prison cells . . .

Chapter 8

Shouts erupted from the Forsaken as a collective understanding took place.

"Traitors!"

"Gods curse you!"

"The boss is gonna skin each and every one of you!"

On they went. Then Dwapek sensed the use of magic, and considered drawing in some of his own, but Sachem Freedek held something up high above his head and said, "Tut, tut."

All eyes went to the blue sapphire of power held up by the Sachem, and the shouting ceased. "We can't have you down here using the power of the gods. That would cause a stir. And of course, I'd be forced to turn the whole lot of you into ash."

One of the Forsaken, Dwapek thought his name might have been Thomas, said, "You're no wielder adept. That stone is no threat while in your hands."

Sachem Freedek rounded on the man. "Are you certain of that? Come on, try me. Give me the excuse." He held up the stone, eyes fixed on the challenger.

Thomas spat, shoulders slumping in defeat.

After a generous pause, Sachem Freedek peeled his glare away from Thomas to share with the rest. He seemed to taste the air before continuing. "Now, I understand your disappointment at the change of plans. I do. But unfortunately, your 'boss' presented his plan to me with little room for negotiation, leaving me few options but to make plans of my own. Plus, that wily old Petregof intended to maintain control of the artifact after this was finished." The Sachem guffawed. "To think, the Naca Omin agreeing to allow one of the Forsaken to maintain control over an artifact of such power! It's unfathomable. Now all will be as it should. And after the Nazca have been wiped from the Valley, and if Petregof behaves, I may even allow the Forsaken some sort of status among the Renziks. We'll see."

He lowered his hand. "Now, if you would all kindly follow the instructions set out by these wonderfully friendly guards, your chances of survival will increase dramatically. I would love to be able to return all of you to your boss as an act of good faith after what he'll likely see as a great betrayal. However, he'll understand the need to eliminate any who have refused to abide by my rules."

Dwapek's legs barely held his weight. *This can't be happening.*

"Move," said someone from behind, accompanied by the point of a spear suddenly pressing into the small of his back.

He was directed to enter one of the more than two dozen cells lining the perimeter of the space. His, like all the others, was cut from the bedrock. Metal bars extended above a waist-high wall that stretched the length of the cell facing the center of the circular room. The steel door swung on creaky hinges, and the bolts that locked each door became an echoey song until Dwapek and the ten others were all secured within their respective holding places.

Curses and murmurs blanketed the room as the Forsaken settled into their new residences, Dwapek among them. He should have seen this coming. Yet even with such foresight, would he have been able to do anything about it? Had there been any point where he could have changed the outcome? Perhaps if he'd headed in the other direction after escaping the sinkhole? But he suspected he would have still found himself in the hands of the Forsaken one way or another if he remained in the Valley. He wondered if he should have just allowed the bear to kill him. At the moment, that seemed like it might have been a better option. Then there was his mother. Had Dwapek simply remained quiet and let the bear attack her, he would still be a member of his tribe, an adult on his way home to be married. But he wouldn't have been able to live with the guilt. He would have hated himself forever.

He fisted his hands and chided himself for languishing in the pointlessness of could-haves. He needed to focus on what was.

Sachem Freedek spoke up. "Now that you're all comfortable, be advised that the use of magic will not be permitted at any point during your stay. Toward that end, I have employed my most trusted and talented Naphtali Shamans to keep an eye on you. They have a special talent for detecting the transfer of energy, as well as the ability to combat it. They will remain here with you, alongside a team of guards with a special proclivity toward violence. Don't test their patience."

Dwapek reached up and gripped the bars of his cell, staring hopelessly out at the rest of the circular room as Sachem Freedek and several of their "escorts" departed. The lighting was limited to four lamps placed evenly around the perimeter of the room. Each cell was filled with gloomy blackness, revealing none of its occupants besides those few like him who had chosen to stand with faces against the bars of their cell.

Holding the metal in his hands, Dwapek dreamed of escape in spite of Freedek's warning. He probed the iron bars with his mind, sensing the residual energy within. He could feel the areas with the most highly concentrated matter as well as those with the least. Even still, destabilizing an unnatural marriage of metal like iron or steel to the point of fragility would be no easy feat. It was too much like a diamond or gem to weaken enough to dissolve. The residual vitality in such objects clung to itself almost as tightly as the energy of living creatures.

His only recourse would be to find and exploit an area of imperfection, draw the excess energy from that precise location, and hope it was weakened enough to bend or break by more traditional means. Not impossible, but unlikely. He attempted to rattle the bars if for no other reason than the satisfaction of hearing the sound of his own resistance to this imprisonment. The metal did not even grant him that.

A voice beside Dwapek startled him. It was low, almost a whisper. "Such a course would not end well."

Dwapek did not recognize the extraordinarily deep voice. "Huh?" he responded.

"The bars. They are well constructed. And the Shamans, well, they would be turning the key to your cell before you even finished your work."

Annoyed by the invasion of his brooding with a statement of the obvious, Dwapek considered denying that he had even thought about escape by such means. Then he thought to argue. But what would be the point? His pride mattered little at this point. He settled on a more intelligent response than either. He grunted.

The shallow voice responded in a gentler tone. "One can hardly blame you for dreaming."

Dwapek looked over to the adjacent cell from which the voice originated. There was no one there. Of course an individual would have to bring his face right up to the bars in order to be seen under such low visibility.

Dwapek was more curious about the owner of the voice than about what he said. There was an accent to his pronunciations and his words seemed more stilted than those spoken by the Forsaken. Were there others down here besides himself and his party?

Dwapek settled on a direct question. "Who are you?"

The man took so long to respond that Dwapek thought the question had either offended or the owner simply hadn't heard him. Just as Dwapek opened his mouth to repeat the question, the man said, "You may call me Targon. And to whom do I have the pleasure of speaking?"

"I am Dwapek." He decided to confirm his suspicion about the man's accent. "You weren't among the Forsaken just imprisoned here, were you? You were already here?"

Targon replied, "I have been here for nearly a full turn of the moon so far as I can guess."

"What did you do to get yourself locked in here?"

"Well, that's just the thing. I'd risked the perilous journey by sea to make trade with your brethren to the north at least a dozen times before, bringing coveted items from the south: rugs from Scritland, sculptures from Kael, and even the occasional enchanted item. You northerners have quite the cache of geodes in these lands, especially within the Valley, and there's quite the demand for such things in the south.

"My men and I were returning from the overland leg of one such expedition when we were ambushed and taken captive by these Naphtali. This coming right on the heels of renegotiated terms to travel these lands. Sachem Freedek himself wished us safe passage before setting out on our journey."

Dwapek understood. "If only Sachem Freedek was a man of his word."

"Indeed," grumbled Targon.

Dwapek was still digesting Targon's mention of the south. "What exactly do you mean by 'the south'? Travel by sea would mean you're from . . ."

"The land of men, yes."

A human? The revelation brought Dwapek back to that painful episode of his youth, to the enchanted knife and his father's disdain. Dwapek's forehead warmed at the thought. He had resented those humans, for without their visit, his father might never have treated Dwapek the way he had. And while Dwapek knew this man should not be held personally responsible for Dwapek's sufferings, he still felt an immediate barrier. Dwapek looked at the wall of solid rock that separated their cells. *Well, another barrier.*

Targon interrupted Dwapek's bubbling anger with a question of his own. "Would you mind joining me toward the back of the cell? These old bones would like to rest."

Dwapek responded, confused by the man's suggestion. "You do realize there is a stone wall between our cells."

"Oh yes, the wall. Right you are. Yet I ask you to indulge me."

Dwapek heard some light shuffling. He stalked back to the corner of his latest residence with little expectation.

But it turned out there was a small hole between the cells. Dwapek put his hand through, then as a reflex checked to see if anything was loose. He tried the top, both sides and the bottom—it moved! He began wriggling it back and forth until the man gave him pause. "It won't do you any good, unless your goal is to draw undue attention to yourself. Escaping into my cell brings you no closer to freedom."

Dwapek removed his hand from the hole and sank against the wall, resigned to his fate here in this cell with a stranger for company.

The man's voice had no difficulty finding its way through the hole in the wall. "So, tell me, Dwapek, I couldn't help but overhear that you and your companions are of the Forsaken."

Targon let the statement linger.

Oh, he's looking for confirmation. "I'm not—well, not really. But I was with them when we were betrayed by Freedek. It seems his tendency to lie is not unusual."

"I see," replied Targon. "I suspect the story of how you and your friends found yourselves at one time in league with Freedek is an interesting one? It is not often that the Renzik tribes have dealings with their kin north of the Veld, am I right?"

Dwapek's stomach tightened. He hesitated to tell the truth about the artifact, about his own sin against the gods. Yet what did it matter? He didn't have the artifact. Who was this human going to tell? They were both destined to hang, burn, or worse.

He felt a weight lift as he told the entire tale, from the bear in the Veld, all the way to the artifact and his betrayal by Sachem Freedek. It felt good to put words to the sequence of events; the injustice of it all seemed only to increase once voiced.

Targon, however, remained silent throughout the telling and Dwapek wondered if he had fallen asleep with disinterest, or perhaps disbelief. Just as Dwapek opened his mouth to inquire, the man said, "Curious . . ."

There was a long pause and Dwapek finally said, "What's curious?"

"Well, perhaps nothing. Just sounds to me like the kind of power you wielded should have left you crippled or dead. If you don't mind my asking, when you wielded the power of this 'stone,' what did it feel like? Did it feel like the volume of power used was proportional to the damage inflicted?"

"I . . . uh . . ." Truth was, he didn't feel like he had wielded the power himself. "It felt . . . I don't know, like there wasn't enough to do what it did." He thought back to his theory about how this worked. "I believe the artifact drew additional power from around me, but didn't channel it directly through me. That would explain how the artifact allows its wielder to use so much energy."

Targon said, "Hmm. I have never heard of the energy of the world working in such a way. Are you certain that you were the only one wielding power during this demonstration?"

Dwapek opened his mouth to respond, *Of course I'm sure*. Given the enhanced ability to sense magic while holding the stone, he was fairly confident about his answer. Except, he knew one's ability to sense magic while wielding was severely diminished. But the question was irrelevant. "I don't understand what you mean."

This man probably doesn't understand magic. It would be easy enough to doubt without having witnessed firsthand the artifact's immense power. He was human, after all.

Targon sighed. "I don't doubt that what you say happened did so precisely the way you describe. It's just . . . I am aware of only a *very* limited number of objects capable of doing as you describe, and these are not objects that can be wielded by just anyone, wielder adept or not." The man remained silent for a time, then added, "Of course, even if I'm correct, there still remains the question of what Petregof gains by having you and Sachem Freedek *believe* that this artifact is so powerful. Why send you to this Naca Omin knowing the artifact will not work during your demonstration? Very curious, indeed."

Dwapek inserted, "Perhaps the artifact is actually what Petregof says it is."

Targon responded, "Mm."

"Listen, I watched Petregof slay a Nazca like he was simply lighting a lamp. I single-handedly disintegrated an entire tree, roots and all. I could never have done that without the artifact."

Targon responded, irritatingly calmly. "Perhaps not. But is there another possibility?"

Dwapek ground his teeth. *Why am I even arguing with this man? What does it matter? Whether we're executed or not, we're not likely to see the light of day again.*

And yet, Dwapek sighed. "All right. I'll play. What is this *other* possibility?"

"What if the power wielded in both instances was not of the artifact at all, but the combined effort of several wielders working in tandem?"

Dwapek scoffed. "That's not possible . . ." *I would have sensed their magic. That is, unless they wielded at the exact same time. But, no. This is ridiculous.*

The man responded, "I have seen it done. If Petregof traveled south to the lands of the humans, he may have learned the secrets of such a practice. It is not an uncommon practice among some of the priesthoods of men."

But this explanation, as fantastical as it sounded, still circled back to the question of why Petregof would go through the trouble of making Dwapek and Sachem Freedek falsely believe the artifact was as powerful as it was. If the artifact was not what he said it was, Dwapek's demonstration before the Naca Omin would fail. Freedek would be made a fool, and Dwapek's being there would be of little consequence. *Why keep me alive, tell me this story, then send me to fail? It makes no sense.* He considered Targon's theory and wondered if the Forsaken might somehow assist in the wielding of the artifact, or if perhaps that had been the plan. Except, no, they would not be anywhere near Dwapek if he might be asked to perform. The timing would also have to be perfect. No, not possible.

Dwapek didn't know why he cared to prove that he was right, that the artifact was real. Maybe to justify the false hope he had felt. To make himself feel like less of a fool for believing . . .

"None of this explains why Petregof would arrange for me to carry the artifact into the Naca Omin, if it's a complete falsehood." He shifted as he spoke and felt his purse, and the bone necklace. *Of course!* Feeling confident in his position, Dwapek said, "Why would Petregof have given me a talisman to protect me from the effects of wielding too much, if not to protect me from effects of wielding the artifact's power?"

Targon said flatly, "Mm. A talisman you say? It seems you failed to mention this."

Dwapek reached into the pocket where he had stowed it and held one of the small bones in his hand. "Right before I left, Petregof called me into his tent and gave me this talisman." He held it up as if to show the man. "He claimed it would give my bones an added layer of protection, in case those in attendance at the Naca Omin required a larger demonstration than killing a Nazca or destroying a tree."

"This talisman. How many gemstones does it contain? And how large are they?"

Dwapek answered, sure that he had finally proven himself right. "It's a necklace, lined with bones. There are a few small gems, as well."

Targon's tone slipped from monotone to . . . something akin to concern. "This talisman wouldn't happen to have a chain crafted from black metal rings, would it?"

Dwapek felt a cloud of cold confusion wash over him. *How could he know?* Then Dwapek figured it out. Relieved. *Targon probably sold this talisman to Petregof.*

Targon was quiet for another spell before finally responding. "It is fortunate for you, and a great many others, that Sachem Freedek betrayed you when he did. I believe Petregof has given to you the Etzem Tzaraath."

The name meant nothing to Dwapek, but the idea that this betrayal was somehow good raked at his nerves. He snapped, "Are you dim or just twisted? There is *nothing* good about my being captive here."

Targon's tone remained unchanged as he continued in an *I know more than you* way that made Dwapek wish to reach through the hole in the wall that separated them and punch him in the throat. Targon said, "Ah, but you see, you are alive right now. And may continue as such so long as you do not wield power while wearing that wretched weapon of plague."

Dwapek ground his teeth, then spoke slowly, firmly. "Allow me to explain again what this talisman is intended to—"

"Oh, I understand precisely what it is intended to do. As does Petregof. *This* is why he has sent you to the Naca Omin: to unleash the vile plague of the Etzem Tzaraath. By the next turn of the moon, much of the Renzik population would be exterminated without Petregof having lifted a finger."

Dwapek started, "What are you—" He threw up his hands in frustration, regardless of the fact that Targon could not see him do so. "You know what. I'm just gonna say it. You're a loon. Plain and simple." Dwapek wondered how long he would be kept captive and how long it would take him to reach the same state of insanity as the man beside him. *Pray they kill me first.*

Targon spoke again as if Dwapek hadn't just twice insulted his mental faculties. "He's going to come for you. Force you to wield its power."

Dwapek couldn't believe the stubbornness of this man's delusions. "Who? The Sachem? He doesn't need me to wield the artifact."

"You're right, but that's only because the artifact is not what you think it is. He'll think he needs you, especially after it fails to produce the results he witnessed before. At that point, he'll believe what Petregof said about your abilities is true. He'll have a few Shamans try first. They will fail. Then he'll come for you, and you will wish to be gone from here when this happens. Or at least not holding the Etzem Tzaraath."

What is his angle? And what did he just call it? Then it struck him.

"Let me guess. You want me to pass the Etze—the talisman over to you? For 'safe' keeping?"

Targon scoffed. "Heavens no. I want nothing to do with that abomination."

Not that, then.

Targon took the opportunity created by Dwapek's silence to explain further. "You and I both know Petregof would never trust that Sachem Freedek wouldn't at least attempt to wield the artifact himself prior to the Naca Omin. And that fact is why Petregof did not provide the Sachem with the true weapon, lest he diminish the effectiveness of the plague by releasing it prior to the Naca Omin. If Petregof succeeds, he'll not only weaken the Renzik tribes themselves, he'll slay their leaders. This done, who would prevent him from swooping in to take control over a weakened Renzik confederation?"

Dwapek nodded, then remembered Targon would not be able to see him. "Yes, I suppose it would. But then, why would Petregof not simply use the talisman himself?"

"Now *that* is a good question. And while I'm not certain of this, some stories suggest that the plague released by the talisman kills even its user. This is an area of dispute among scholars, as some stories describe the user of the Etzem Tzaraath as walking among the dead like an undertaker, while others say the user perishes with the rest. Who is to say the truth, but I rather believe it is the latter."

Dwapek grew more irritated by the minute. So what if this man somehow discerned the design of the necklace? That didn't mean it was a weapon of great evil. "How can you presume to know anything about the intentions of the leader of the Forsaken?" Dwapek didn't want to believe that he had been deceived by both Petregof and Freedek. If that was true, then he had no chance of surviving the next few days. None. Petregof *had* to be telling the truth. Had to be.

Targon responded as evenly as ever. "I have read the stories, likely the very same that inspired Petregof to seek this talisman in the first place. The particular event in question comes from a war several thousand years past between the Asaaven and the Luguinden tribes. The Asaaven were a once great civilization, but a nation in decline, while the Luguinden tribes, once united in war, had superior numbers and, worse, unveiled dark sorcery the likes of which had never before been realized in this world. By the end of the war, the Asaaven had been reduced to a mere shadow of a shadow. Still they fought, and before their final demise, they unleashed dark magic of their own: a parting gift before the remnants of their people faded into obscurity."

Dwapek scoffed. "Legends and myths."

Targon replied, "Perhaps. Nonetheless, some accounts from those who survived were quite detailed. The power of their words have inspired grave robbers and worse to risk defiling the sites of these battles in the Hand of the Gods in search of such a weapon. Of course, it is entirely possible that Petregof simply found something that *looks* like what is described in these stories. There exists no shortage of dark-alley merchants willing to sell such things to desperate clients. Yet something tells me Petregof would have found a way to test this weapon before believing in its capabilities."

Dwapek felt a chill enter the room. The dead he and his tribe had passed on their way to the Veld . . .

"So let's pretend for a moment that you're not a total ice-brain. What would you suggest I do when Sachem Freedek comes down here and forces me to wield his pretend weapon of power?"

Targon responded, "If I am correct about his intentions, I would be certain not to touch the Etzem Tzaraath while you wield any amount of magic. Any at all. To do so would mean the deaths of everyone and everything around, including yourself. The more magic you wield, the larger the path of destruction."

"So instead of protecting myself from permanent injury while wielding the artifact, I should *not* protect myself, but still wield the artifact, which you say will fail to produce the results Freedek expects." Dwapek shook his head. "I die either way." The realization stirred feelings of renewed frustration. There was no way out.

"Even a prison has doors."

Dwapek glowered. "And prisoners are at the mercy of their jailers to open them."

"I have rarely seen a prison with only one entrance. And the thing about entrances . . . they also serve as exits."

The man is mad. Plain and simple, mad.

"Before you go, might I suggest one final word of advice?"

Dwapek took in a deep breath of sarcasm before responding, "Oh, please do," rolling his eyes in spite of the darkness.

"Should you ever find yourself in need of refuge, there is a small port to the northwest, a trade outpost of men. If I were a Renzik in search of escape, that is where I would go. There are places in the southern lands where even Renzikken wielders like you might find acceptance."

"Uh-huh, thank you for that."

Dwapek scooted his bottom and pivoted so he could lie down. He was exhausted, body and mind alike. He closed his eyes, hoping for a few hours of rest before he was summoned to do Freedek's bidding.

The creak of a door echoed from beyond the cell and Dwapek was suddenly awake. *Wh-what time is it? Where am . . . ?* It all came back in a flash of discomforting memories. He sat up and peered beyond his cell in time to see Sachem Freedek enter the circular prison. Dwapek's heart pounded as the Renzik leader made a direct line toward him. "Open this cell—now," he commanded.

One of Freedek's lackeys sprang to his feet and Dwapek was suddenly without time to weigh his options. Did he listen to a man he'd just met, a presumed criminal from the world beyond, or believe the word of one of the Forsaken? It was like being given the choice between execution by poison or spear.

He looked up and saw Freedek only a few paces away, closing quickly the distance between himself and Dwapek's cell. As it was, the talisman was not in direct contact with his skin, and if he was going to act, he needed to do so now. He reached into his pocket and gripped the talisman, the Etzem Tzaraath, as Targon had called it.

He felt the smooth bones around the black metallic circlet and started to pull it free. It was dark in this cell, perhaps dark enough to hide the weapon in the corner, at least for now. But what then? Someone would find it and report it to Freedek even if they didn't know what it was. What would happen then? Perhaps that would be better than Dwapek using it at the Naca Omin. He pulled the talisman free and moved his hand behind him, his knuckles touching the cold, dark stone shaping the corner of the cell.

Keys jingled in the lock and Dwapek knew he was out of time. He returned his fist to his side and slid the talisman back into the hidden pocket of his cloak.

Sachem Freedek addressed him in a jovial tone, as if Dwapek had been staying as a guest in a neighboring tent. "Dwapek, it's time for you to show everyone just how special you are."

Dwapek whispered into the hole that separated his cell from Targon's. "Let us pray you were wrong."

Targon whispered back, "Brushes with death from which we survive are often worth two lives."

Dwapek had no idea what that was supposed to mean. He rose to his feet and started toward his captor, pondering Targon's strange words, wondering how much longer he had left to live. *Days? Hours? . . .*

Chapter 9

Dwapek's mouth was clammy and dry, his hands sweaty, and his heart thumped like a hammer in his chest as the red-painted mammoth tent of the Naca Omin came into view.

Sachem Freedek paused, and turned to face Dwapek. "You will do precisely as you are told, speak precisely when you are told, breathe precisely when and how you are told. Demons below, you'd best only think what you are told. Is that understood?"

"Well, I suppose that depends."

Freedek's eyes narrowed. "Careful."

Dwapek swallowed a mouthful of fear. "What happens to me after this is all said and done? Because if you're intending to send me back to that cell to rot, then you may as well kill me now."

Dwapek figured his odds of being punched were pretty good, and he tensed in anticipation.

Freedek, however, surprised him with a rare smile. "Stones, indeed. Stones, indeed. Nevertheless, what happens next depends on your level of compliance. Should you do precisely what you're told, I will uphold my end of the bargain. Disobey me, and you'll meet a most slow and painful death. My Shamans will work to keep you alive for as long as possible throughout your torture to extend your suffering."

Dwapek swallowed fear-flavored bile, then nodded. "That seems perfectly reasonable."

Freedek's expression returned to its customary scowl. "Good. Now it is time."

As they approached the tent, Dwapek decided to gamble on a final question. "Sachem, just out of curiosity, how many of your Shamans attempted to wield the stone, you know, before you decided to snatch me from my cell to do what they could not?"

A flash of *something* fell upon Freedek's expression, but it was brief and Dwapek wasn't sure exactly what it meant. The Renzik issued no verbal response. By this time they had come within a few strides of the entrance to the tent, where a pair of Renziks holding tall spears stood at attention. A nod from Freedek cued them to pull open the flap on either side to allow Dwapek and his captor to step through.

Dwapek's eyes were immediately drawn to the small pile of coals glowing at the center of a ring of dark, wooden chairs carved from thick tree stumps. The seat furthest from the entrance was the largest and most ornate with glyphs and other designs carved into it. The other six were simple, uniform in size and shape, and each occupied by a Renzik Sachem, save one, presumably for Sachem Freedek. There was a seventh seat, though it was more like a wooden perch, a stump. *I suppose I should be thankful I'm afforded a seat at all,* thought Dwapek. The Renziks rose in greeting, as Sachem Freedek approached, though there was nothing warm in their expressions.

Dwapek followed and almost stopped midstride the moment he met the eyes of his father, which widened in shock before quickly narrowing in anger. This reunion would be just as hostile as Dwapek expected. Sachem Aldrek remained standing while the others took their seats. His tone was biting as he said, "What are you playing at, Freedek? This . . . this—he is cursed. He broke the silence of the hunt. His attendance is an affront to the gods, an affront to this most sacred meeting. I demand he be removed and banished immediately. I vow an oath on my life that I witnessed the event in question with my own eyes."

Dwapek had stopped moving, frozen in place as he awaited his fate, his legs feeling like they were carrying several times his weight.

Sachem Freedek smiled, and calmly gestured for Dwapek to be seated in the small chair beside the largest of the seats before which he now stood. "This young Renzik is a guest of the hosting Sachem of this Naca Omin. Tell me, Aldrek, where in our sacred law does it specify any such limitations on who or what I bring to speak on matters of importance?"

Aldrek's face grew red and Dwapek half expected him to draw a weapon. "I . . . well . . . there is no such preclusion." He raised a finger. "But the only reason such a one was not included was because our founders never foresaw such disrespectful idiocy coming from a Sachem, of all people!"

Sachem Freedek seated himself, outwardly unconcerned with Aldrek's fury.

Aldrek continued, "The solution is simple. I as Sachem of Tribe Danswa put forth that any non-Renzik member of society be barred from attending the Naca Omin, even as guest, including this very session."

Dwapek noticed a few heads nodding, but Freedek raised a hand, index finger waggling back and forth as he tsked. "As this year's host, I have right of first refusal to present to the council. Considering your response to my guest's presence here, I think it prudent to exercise this right, don't you? You are of course welcome to introduce this act to the council once the circle reaches you, but I suspect after everyone hears what I have to say, and sees what my guest can do, you will stand alone in your objection."

Aldrek extended his own finger toward Freedek. "You hide behind the law like pestilence to a corpse."

Dwapek squirmed at the use of such an analogy. He reached his hand into the hidden pocket and felt the talisman. *Targon is a madman. Nothing more.*

Freedek was now the only one standing. "We are naught but savages without the law, my friend. Now, if you are quite finished, I would like this 756th meeting of the Naca Omin to commence."

With no audible objections, Freedek raised both hands, palms facing the canvas roof of the tent that extended toward a central hole and began to pray.

"Earthmother, you breathed life into the world, and through your hand all things are made possible. I ask that you bless this meeting of the chosen few, that we might bring your strength and protection to all the realm."

This was little different than the prayers Aldrek had spoken before his tribe. Mumbles of affirmation were followed by silence as everyone raised their heads in anticipation of what Sachem Freedek and his cursed guest had in store for them.

Several more ceremonial words of deference and reverence to the gods were spoken, and some sort of powder was thrown upon the coals, causing them to glow green instead of red, then all was silent and Sachem Freedek asked Dwapek to stand.

"I stand before you with the answer to our greatest struggle. I am prepared to shatter centuries of tradition built upon the reality that the Nazca would ravage our homes and loved ones, should we ever attempt to settle the Valley of Nar. Here I am with the solution."

He gestured toward Dwapek, who felt his shoulders sag with the gravity of such a claim, praying that he would prove worthy. The whispers from the Sachems around the circle only increased Dwapek's doubts. He heard whispers, of "Absurd. Impossible. Madness."

Dwapek could hardly disagree with them.

"I know what you're all thinking. I, too, believed this was true, but I do not expect you to trust mere words." He pulled the artifact from a pocket in his coat and held the marbled blue object up high, the green light of the coals giving the stone an aquamarine appearance.

"My honored guest has proven himself a wielder adept, easily outperforming my most skilled Shaman, Ygrett. Just one week past, I watched with my own eyes as the ground was painted with Nazca blood and guts without the use of a single spear. I watched as this boy disintegrated an entire megala tree, roots and all. I now implore you to witness a demonstration, so you might believe in the future that is to come. A future that includes permanent settlement within the Valley of Nar. Should he fail to impress, I relinquish the rest of my time and right of refusal for the remainder of the Naca Omin. I also vow to throw an affirming vote to all other proposals presented during this most sacred meeting."

Dwapek looked about the room, watching the expressions of doubt turn into consideration, then nods of approval. Freedek had presented them with an opportunity to gain, no matter the outcome. Everyone appeared happy to agree except, of course, Sachem Aldrek.

He raised a hand. "May I speak?"

Sachem Freedek's expression conveyed annoyance, but he agreed, knowing he had the votes to proceed no matter Aldrek's objections.

Aldrek grinned. "You say this known defiler is a wielder adept. I say he is not. And while I'm not certain of your plan for 'demonstrating' the power of this artifact, I for one would place more trust in a demonstration selected by someone else." He paused for effect. "This is of course in no way a suggestion that you might 'tamper' with something you have had weeks, perhaps months to devise . . ."

"Of course not," growled a scowling Freedek.

"Still, I would rest easier knowing that this demonstration had more of an improvised structure, more like what the boy might experience in the Valley of Nar, should your words prove true."

"Okay, well, get on with it," said an impatient Freedek.

Dwapek had been uneasy about the situation before, not that he had any choice in the matter. But knowing that his father was devising a plan of his own exacerbated his concerns. Whatever his father would propose would be far more dangerous than Freedek's plan. He cringed as Aldrek held up his index finger to silence the room once more.

Aldrek raised both hands. "The Naphtali have always been well regarded for their *unique* methods of delivering the gods' justice by way of the Crixus."

Dwapek sucked in a breath that nearly caused him to choke. The Crixus was a combat arena that placed the fate of the accused into the hands of the gods, or so it was said. The reality was, the Crixus provided cruel entertainment as the Naphtali watched those accused of crimes be butchered to death by captured animals or other trained fighters. The odds were always stacked against the accused and the outcome was rarely far from glorified execution.

Aldrek had the attention of the entire room, everyone leaning forward, intrigued by his mention of the Crixus. They knew where this was going, as did Dwapek.

"You are confident that this object will allow the boy to slay a Nazca with no difficulty, yes?"

Freedek nodded. "That is what I have said."

Aldrek nodded. "Then surely he would have no difficulty demonstrating its power on a lesser threat?"

Sachem Freedek raised an eyebrow but responded, "Of course."

"Well, if the rumors are to be believed, the Crixus currently boasts a creature that has carried out a record eighty-seven sentences of the accused since being captured just five moons past, each criminal armed with a spear and shield. This is true?"

Sachem Freedek nodded, eyes betraying his concern over where this was going.

"I propose we let the gods decide if the boy and the rock are indeed worthy of our attention. Surely, if he can make a Nazca disappear, he'll have no trouble vanquishing a comparably mild creature."

Expressions of approval blossomed around the room. Sachem Lephrem of Tribe Mana chuckled. "I could use some entertainment. I'm in support."

Others followed and Sachem Freedek knew he would be a fool to think he could steer this ship elsewhere. He nodded. "This can be arranged, yes?"

Aldrek added, "To be clear, the boy will have no weapon besides the stone. It is, after all, the power of the stone that must be proved, yes?"

Aldrek's words were laden with an all-too-familiar smugness. This was bad. Very bad.

Sachem Freedek nodded and maintained a neutral tone as he said, "We have reached consensus on the matter, so if there is nothing else, I declare this 756th meeting of the Naca Omin adjourned until the outcome of this trial has concluded."

Freedek paused as he waited for the obligatory ayes of approval to subside. "Very well. I will make the necessary preparations. The event will take place within the Crixus as soon as it can be arranged."

Everything dimmed, and though Dwapek had just come to his feet, he lowered himself into his chair as the room started to spin. He was not built for this sort of thing. The hot air wafting up to his nose from the coals threatened to choke his lungs, his ears were filled with an eerie ringing, and his vision swam in circles. A gentle hand squeezed his shoulder and the overwhelming weight of the moment lifted.

Sachem Freedek's voice whispered into his ear. "One way or another, it will all be over soon."

Dwapek was not comforted.

Dwapek had been unable to catch a glimpse of Targon when originally summoned from the cell. However, as he was returned to await his "trial by wielding," he couldn't help but try. But as he approached, he saw no one. *Must still be hiding in the corner.* The area toward the back closest to his own cell was obscured by darkness. Dwapek veered to his left to have a look, but still, no one. Though he couldn't be certain because of the heavy gloom. Dwapek's stomach sank.

"Sachem, what happened to the man who was in the cell beside mine. Is he still there?"

Freedek stopped and looked at Dwapek, an expression of genuine confusion. "Who?"

"The man who was imprisoned in this cell right here," said Dwapek as he pointed.

The Sachem paused for just a moment before shuffling Dwapek into his cell. "There hasn't been a prisoner on *either* side of your cell since you arrived."

Perhaps he doesn't keep close tabs on every prisoner. Plus, he's been traveling.

"Can you ask one of the guards? Please."

Freedek rolled his eyes. "Hedren. Have there been any prisoners in cell four or six this week?"

A portly, long-bearded Renzik turned and answered, "No, Sachem. No prisoners in either cell for quite some time. We've kept this place as empty as possible, on your order."

Sachem Freedek turned and remarked, "Satisfied?"

Dwapek shook his head. "His name was Targon." He spoke loud enough for Hedren to hear. "A human. He called himself Targon."

Hedren shook his head. "I'm certain I would remember *that!* A human prisoner?"

Sachem Freedek locked the cell door and chuckled. "Don't go losing your mind on me now. I need—and more importantly, *you* need—to perform. Get some rest. Tomorrow is going to be an eventful day."

Dwapek felt light-headed as he shuffled to the back of the cell. He sank to the cold stone floor in the exact location he'd sat while speaking with Targon, whose voice he recalled so vividly. Could that have been some sort of stress-induced dream? If not, why lie about the prisoner? Neither made sense, but both seemed equally likely.

"Why indeed," whispered Dwapek.

Chapter 10

Immersed in complete darkness beneath the arena floor of the famed Crixus, Dwapek stood on shaky legs. This place was well known for its role in the butchery of Naphtali criminals. Dwapek had no desire to join their ranks. He listened intently to the muffled sound of someone above addressing the crowd of onlookers, but could not make out any words.

He held in his sweaty palm the only means by which he might escape whatever lay in wait for him. In the chaos of preparations, Sachem Freedek had left Dwapek under the care of guards who seemed unwilling to speak of whatever it was that awaited him. All he knew for sure was that the creature he would be confronting had laid waste to the nearly one hundred Renziks it had faced, and they'd been armed.

Clasping the smooth blue stone in his hand, he prayed it would be enough to protect him. A trumpet sounded from above and the floor began to shake. His stomach pushed bile into his throat and his legs trembled with nervous energy.

He'd never been to this arena, but his father had taken him to witness Naphtali "justice" the last time the Naca Omin had been hosted here. The arena had been nothing more than a circular pit in the ground surrounded by a wooden railing to keep spectators from falling in. Dwapek had watched as a team of Renzik warriors butchered the accused, a serial thief. It had lasted longer than it should have, and Dwapek had taken ill.

Spears of light exploded on all four sides of the ceiling and the cage groaned as it moved ever upward, toward the sand floor of the Crixus. Dwapek closed his eyes against the sudden brightness and the shouts raining down on him from the crowd. It seemed the short notice of the event had not affected attendance. The crank of the lift stopped and Dwapek slowly opened his eyes, shielding them from the bright afternoon light. The inner arena was a deep depression carved entirely from dark-brown stone, while the elevated seating was built of wood, benches extending dozens of rows above. Every seat was filled.

Dwapek took a wobbly step forward, his moccasins sinking into the thick, dry sand of the arena floor. The light-tan grains were speckled and crusty with the blood of the condemned. Dwapek looked from side to side, but saw no foe. For some reason, that felt worse. *Let's just get this over with.*

He held the blue stone in one hand while he reached into the pocket of his coat to feel the bones of the talisman, still haunted by the warning given to him by Targon.

I will either be the hero of my people, or I will ruin them all. In either case, Petregof would be right about one thing: Dwapek might change the future of their people forever.

A bone-chilling roar blasted from behind and Dwapek spun to face the source, dropping the stone as he did. He sank to his knees as he turned to face the source of the bestial war cry of—

A silvertip bear as it released another roar.

Another bear? Oh, the irony.

Dwapek scrambled backward on his hands and knees, watching in horror as the monstrous bear lunged forward and swiped with his head-sized paw. Oohs and ahs from the crowd accompanied the metallic clink of iron as a chain flexed. Sand sprayed as the interconnected metal rings lifted from the ground, and Dwapek was relieved to see that the silvertip was, for the moment, restrained. Each link was nearly as thick as Dwapek's wrists.

Dwapek's left palm found the cold stone of the artifact and he gripped it tight as he came to his feet just a few paces away from the menacing creature of the gods' justice.

The crowd quieted and Dwapek saw motion to his right. A Renzik stood, arms raised. It was Sachem Freedek. "We are gathered to witness history. Below, you see—"

"Nice pun!" shouted a spectator from the other side.

That resulted in a few chuckles from the assembled until someone else yelled out. "That's not a pun, you idiot! It's literally below." The crowd erupted in laughter.

Sachem Freedek silenced the crowd with his hands. "Peace, brothers and sisters. Peace. The only violence anyone is here to see will take place in the ring."

The silvertip growled and shook its head from side to side, putting the chain to the test once more.

Sachem Freedek continued, his tone unconcerned. "The Renzik standing within the Crixus alongside Maul is here to demonstrate the gift of the gods to our people."

Maul? They call him Maul? Good God, I'm going to die.

"I am not at liberty to speak further on the matter until the conclusion of the Naca Omin. But I assure you, this will mark a new age in these lands. A departure from darkness. So, without further ado . . ."

That's when Dwapek noticed the four smaller shapes, Renziks, behind the chained beast. They were fastening metal clasps to a thick metal anchor in the stone floor of the arena. Finished, they fled down a ramp on the other side of the arena, which Dwapek suspected would disappear once they had reached safety.

Dwapek fingered the talisman in his pocket, knowing he needed to summon the power of the stone any second or be mangled before he had the chance. *Do I trust Petregof or the ghost from the cell?* To choose wrong meant certain death in one case, and in the other . . .

An epiphany struck. *I didn't need the talisman to destroy the tree. The talisman is only meant to protect me in case I summon too much power.* He let the talisman sink back into his pocket then summoned the energy held within the stone. The latent vitality of the gem flowed to him like air to lungs. And not a moment too soon, for this time when the bear pulled on the chains, they dragged easily behind it. Maul was free.

Dwapek held the stone high as he basked in the magic he had drawn. *Now, what do with it?*

Recalling the powerful claws of the silvertip from what felt like years earlier, Dwapek recognized that he had only a moment to act. He allowed the energy he had summoned to coalesce, but instead of pressing it into his limbs to strengthen them as he had with the spear throw, he focused on the idea of that energy compressing into a narrow area outside himself. He extended his free hand toward the barreling creature, trying to ignore the thunder he felt at his feet with each lumbering step. Then he released a blast of raw power.

The stone flashed blue and a wave of power slammed into the silvertip's chest. Maul was knocked off course, though his momentum carried him several paces further. A heap of muscle and fur slammed to the ground, kicking up a spray of sand and dust. The crowd oohed and ahhed at the action.

Dwapek, on the other hand, was less than impressed. While he knew he had just wielded a vast sum of power, more than he could have without the stone to be sure, he did not feel the accompanying power he had felt before. It certainly didn't leave the kind of residual footprint he'd felt after Petregof had sprayed Nazca ichor everywhere.

As if in answer to his doubts, the silvertip groaned a low rumble, then rose to all fours once more, appearing dazed by the blast but otherwise unharmed. Dwapek shuffled to his right then backed away, toward the stone barrier.

The arena was only about forty paces across. Which meant there was nowhere to hide. The wall was too high for him to climb, and Maul's chains, he suspected, would be just long enough for him to kill his prey, but not long enough to allow him to escape into the crowd above.

What have I done wrong? Dwapek drew upon residual energy stored within the stone once again and felt it swell within him, but after having already expended a great deal of power just moments earlier, he felt the strain as the stone began to resist. Did this stone have limits? Of course. But this seemed no different than an ordinary gemstone. This possibility struck him at the same moment the silvertip renewed its interest in him. Maul let out a bellow, stirring the crowd into a frenzy of cheers, before bounding toward Dwapek once again. Far less confident now than he had been the first time, Dwapek held the stone before him and gripped what energy he had been able to summon, still a significant amount, at least according to his pre–Valley of Nar standards.

The blast of power missed the bear completely, but wasn't a complete loss. It struck the ground just in front of the beast, sending a spray of sand and stone into Maul's face. The diversion also caused the bear to lose its balance as his front paws landed on uneven ground.

Dwapek, however, had been so concerned about the magical side of his defense that he failed to react to the physical. While the silvertip was more focused on remaining upright than eating, his momentum carried him right to the place where Dwapek stood. At the last moment, Dwapek's body recognized this problem. He managed one step to his right before the mountain of fur and flesh struck him like a hammer to an anvil.

His head snapped back before his body slammed into the ground, making the moment his face collided with the sand all the more dizzying. He saw stars but didn't have time to linger. With spots swimming before his eyes, Dwapek scrambled to his feet.

Daring a look behind him, he saw the silvertip rising back to all fours, head swinging from side to side to remove the sand that had taken up residence on his long snout. Dwapek continued to run, but he was in a circular arena with no hope of escape. He stopped and turned at the same time the silvertip ended its tirade against the sand. His yellow eyes locked on Dwapek, who glared back. Still clutching the stone, Dwapek knew that he had either failed to utilize it correctly, or it was as Targon suspected, and this was not the mythical stone of power Petregof had professed. In either case, Dwapek had already summoned more than any Renzik should be capable of. He didn't yet feel the ache in his bones, but oftentimes the effects would be delayed. He may have already exceeded a safe limit. To attempt another brute-force attack could be suicide, no matter the outcome with the bear.

Except . . . he reached into his pocket and felt the talisman. This was precisely the sort of situation where something like it would be helpful. The silvertip began moving toward him, this time stalking like a snow leopard, its eyes never leaving Dwapek's.

He gripped the talisman tight enough that he worried he might snap the chain. *I've no other choice.* He extended his mind into the stone held in his other hand, but whatever residual energy remained clung to itself like a mother might a child. Dwapek would not be able to wrest any of its remaining power. He stepped backward, a slow retreat that would fail to match the casual forward progress of the silvertip.

Dwapek feared to end eye contact with Maul lest that action cause the creature to attack more suddenly. *I need more time. But for what? To delay the inevitable?*

The crowd had gone mostly silent, but one onlooker jeered, "Just eat the traitor already!" This was followed by a chorus of assent.

Feeling the cold bones in his hand, Dwapek momentarily hoped Targon was right about the talisman. *These people don't deserve to live.* He drove his mind into the stone beneath his feet. The power stored here was vast. *Perhaps if I target the blast of energy at a single point, the effects might be more severe.* Dwapek imagined a spear of power slamming into the bear's open mouth. *That could work.*

He looked out into the crowd of blood-thirsty patrons, all cheering for his untimely demise. His eye stopped at one onlooker in particular, a figure standing in the back, apart from the rest, towering over all others; a giant, a human.

As striking as a human beside Renziks might be, this was not what lifted the hairs on the back of Dwapek's neck. It was instead the stark contrast between the animated Renziks in the crowd who hooted and hollered with arms raised, and the human's utter stillness. His features were obscured by a deep hood, but Dwapek knew with certainty that this man was staring directly at him, into him. Then the hooded figure raised his hand and pointed at Dwapek and the hood moved from side to side. *What? What do you want? Or not want?*

Dwapek clutched the talisman. *No.* He couldn't wait any longer. But the words of Targon raked at his mind. Except, Targon hadn't been real, had he? Those words were, therefore, false. And yet the memory of the corpses he had found on his way to Veld, twisted by torment, caused his stomach to tighten. That had been *very* real. *Can I risk killing everyone here? Perhaps everyone gathered in this region?* The macabre nature of the mob of spectators hungry for blood did not make guilty the entire Renzik people, did it? The bear continued to stalk, closer with every step even as Dwapek continued to move back in a slight circle.

His hand trembled. *I don't want to die.*

Squeezing harder, his mind gripped the vast reserves of power at his disposal. He imagined the spray of blood as a blade of summoned energy shot through Maul's mouth and out the back of his skull. Yet he had failed to wield the stone. What would happen to him should he somehow survive this trial in the arena? *There will be no victory here for anyone but those who thirst for blood.*

As his hand slipped from the talisman, his grip on the energy of the stone flitted away. He would not survive another large expenditure of magic, and the idea of killing an animal of such great might sickened him. He'd rather perish alone.

In the crowd, the towering hooded figure seemed to nod his approval.

Who are you?

Maul growled, causing Dwapek to return his eyes to the bear. When he looked back to the crowd a moment later, the hooded figure was nowhere to be seen.

Dwapek stopped moving backward. He was finished, resigned to his fate. If a bear was capable of offering an expression of curiosity, it did so now. The muscles above his eyes flexed while his fearsome maw hung slack, no malice but the implied power of his sharp teeth. Yet the silvertip continued to advance, now only a few paces away.

An idea bloomed in Dwapek's mind, albeit an unlikely one. But what was the risk? He was bound for death one way or the other.

Feeling the stone at his feet, Dwapek drove his mind into it and took hold of what he needed; a sliver compared with what he had previously summoned. He drew it in, then extended his mind toward the bear's, which shrank away at his touch. Then it thundered back with such force that Dwapek thought he had been physically assaulted. A moment later, his body was sent sailing helplessly through the air, swatted by Maul's paw like a common fly.

Dwapek landed hard on his side atop the sandy floor, skidding painfully along the ground until coming to rest against the stone barrier of the arena. He was at least glad for modest padding provided by his thick animal-skin jacket and the leather jerkin beneath.

Shaking off disorientation, Dwapek determined to try again. Placing his hands on the stone wall behind him, he drew in another thread of energy, then sent his mind after the bear. This time he pushed past the initial wall of outer rage before hitting another layer of will every bit as imposing as the first. But he sensed something different about this one. While the first mental barrier had been composed of anger and rage, this layer was constructed almost entirely of something unexpected: fear. The emotional strength of this barrier was such that the mere act of touching it with his mind caused him to shrink away as Maul's fear began leaching into him.

He shuddered as the bear stood up on its hind legs and roared, a carnal cry.

In spite of the thick fur, Dwapek could see a number of scars along the bear's underside. Other suspected criminals were likely given spears and swords while facing Maul in the arena. That explained the fear.

But if Dwapek could somehow convince the bear that he was not an enemy . . .

The ability to impress upon an animal's emotions was a primary skill taught to all Renziks, though not everyone had an aptitude for it. Rabbits were particularly easy to soothe, as long as one was able to reach them before fear took hold. Their minds were thin and simplistic. What he felt from Maul was nuanced, a layer of complex interconnected feelings. Dwapek probed this layer of mental fear that prevented him from affecting the bear's emotions, hoping to find a thinner portion to slide past, but he was rebuffed at every turn.

Maul let out another roar, then brought his massive claws down upon the sand, renewing his approach. He stalked toward Dwapek, teeth bared, eyes fixed upon his prey. *This is it,* thought Dwapek. *Earthmother, please, just let it be swift.* He closed his eyes as Maul drew near and flinched as the ground shook just a handsbreadth away from his moccasined foot.

Instinct brought his arms up over his head in mock protection, knowing it would only delay the inevitable. He battled the urge to protect himself, slowly returning his hands to his sides, offering himself to the monster in hopes of a swift end.

Dwapek's entire body trembled. He had been an arrogant fool to think he could affect the mind of a silvertip bear, to think he could do what trained Shamans could not. Wielder adept or no, he was going to be an afternoon snack.

In this moment of acceptance, the strange words of the mysterious prisoner, Targon, resurfaced. *Brushes with death from which we survive are often worth two lives.*

Confounding as these words might be, they brought him back to his last encounter with a silvertip, his last brush with death. He had communed with the other silvertip for only a moment, but during that time, a most intimate memory had been shared. He prayed that would be enough.

Instead of sending his will hurtling toward the bear's mental barrier like a dull spear against stone, Dwapek projected outward the very same images Big Paw had shared with him. He closed his eyes as Maul's massive paw descended.

Chapter 11

Nothing happened. Or at least not the something Dwapek expected. He shuddered as the mighty roar of the silvertip poured over him, a mist of rank breath and saliva tickled at his fledgling beard, his eyes still closed.

A snort followed by another roar and Dwapek dared look, ever so slowly, just in time to get knocked in the side of the head by Maul. He toppled to the side, catching a mouthful of sand. He coughed and spit, then looked up at the bear, confused. The strike had not been the kind meant to injure, not for an undefeated man-eating bear like Maul.

Dwapek sat up without breaking eye contact, then rose to his feet. If a bear was capable of glaring, this one was doing so, along with the low rumbling growl. But Maul wasn't eating him yet; that was good.

TO WIELD A PLAGUE 137

The crowd grew anxious. Words of encouragement like, "Just bite his head off already!" peppered the cheers and jeers of the mob.

"What are you doing?" asked Dwapek.

Maul continued to glare at him, then slammed his paw down on the ground at Dwapek's feet. *What does he want?*

Dwapek had shared with Maul the mental images shared with him by Big Paw during their moment of communion: a mother attacked, her cubs taken from her before their time. This act appeared to have postponed Maul's dinner plans for the time being, but indefinitely? Dwapek needed something more.

Drawing in the power invested in the bedrock and sand around him, he focused his mind on the memory of his own time spent in comfort with Big Paw. Her warmth had been the only reason he survived the night, after all.

He projected his memories of lying tucked into the soft, warm fur of the bear. Maul's blocky head tilted to the side and the next sound was neither angry nor frightening.

Is a friend of a friend a friend? wondered Dwapek.

Dwapek impressed upon Maul the emotions of safety and trust. He met no resistance this time. Feeling around at the edges of the bear's mind, he sensed no openings, but he also experienced none of the anger from before. That was a good sign. *What's my end game? Can there be a draw in the Crixus?* What would happen if

Dwapek simply didn't die? He was pretty sure he knew the answer. Freedek would have him killed, believing he had refused to use the stone.

Something struck Maul in the shoulder. *What the—?*

An angry shout from the crowd. "Come on. Kill 'im an' be done with it!"

This was followed by another fist-sized projectile, which struck Maul square in the skull.

Oh no!

The calm that Dwapek had carefully cultivated vanished in an instant, replaced with carnal rage. The bear rose on his hind legs and released a roar that could be mistaken for nothing less than a battle cry.

Great. This is great. Back to dinner plans. Unless . . .

Is it possible to project the concept of imagination? He had no idea. With nothing to lose but his life, he figured it was worth trying. He drove his consciousness toward Maul once again, this time projecting an idea of something yet to be, a possible future. One he hoped the bear would understand and accept. Dwapek focused all of his will into the thought, then slammed it into the mind of the wrath-filled creature.

Maul stopped where he was, then slowly looked up and growled. The crowd cheered, excited to finally see some sport. The bear pounced.

Nooo!

The giant paws landed just in front of Dwapek, but stopped there. Then Maul lowered himself to the ground and Dwapek sighed in relief. *It worked! It really worked!*

He slipped the blue stone into the pocket alongside the talisman and ran around to the backside of Maul and leaped. His hands gripped a handful of thick fur each and he shimmied his way up the silvertip's mighty hind end.

Maul's entire body shook as he released a powerful roar. Dwapek froze, then realized it was directed not at him.

Phew.

A few disparaging comments had quickly grown into an arena filled with booing patrons. Shouts of anger were followed by the throwing of food and any other projectiles. A fist-sized butt-end of bread careened toward Dwapek's head and he ducked, only to be struck by something else from behind. *Time to go.*

Dwapek sat between Maul's massive, muscular shoulders, hands reaching forward to clasp the iron collar. A chain as thick as Dwapek's wrists still hung to the ground, connected to four others. Something would need to be done about this. *How fast does the stone restore its residual energy?* Pulling it out, he began feeling for the power within and was surprised to find a significant amount.

Sachem Freedek's voice sounded above the din of the arena. "There you go! Now just kill the thing already!"

Dwapek had a much better idea. *Maybe.*

He drove his mind into the cast iron chain that kept Maul's movement limited to the arena. Mapping the chain in his mind's eye, he searched. If he could find and exploit a single imperfection . . . *there!* It was only a minor crack, the beginning of the beginning of something that might someday need to be addressed. Dwapek was going to accelerate this process.

The metal resisted as he continued to draw from a specific line of weakness until nothing further could be pulled from the metal. He hoped this would be enough. *What to do with this energy?* The destabilization would not be complete until the power was actually expended.

Dwapek pushed the energy he had drawn directly into the same place from which he had drawn. That was how many Shamans started fires. As he pushed the energy into the metal, its temperature would rise and it would become more malleable. He watched in wonder as the metal began to glow bloodred, then cherry, orange, yellow, and finally white. *This might work!* But the fur nearest the link was beginning to smoke, and Maul appeared none too pleased. He growled, and Dwapek knew he only had moments before his plan imploded.

Maul rose on his hind legs as Dwapek expended the last of what he had drawn from the metal. Before falling backward off the bear, Dwapek reached up and caught the iron collar around Maul's neck. He hung from his free hand, while the other replaced the stone in his pocket. *This is not what I had in mind.*

And the chain was still intact. *Not enough.* The metal had warped and still glowed bright orange where he had heated it. It had to be close to its breaking point. Just needed a little more help. Without further consideration, Dwapek swung his body over and released his grip on the collar. He allowed himself to fall past the heated portion of the dangling chain before reaching out to catch one of the links in his hand. His body swung outward with his momentum, but the chain held. *Still not enou—*

The tension vanished and he was suddenly falling, his head rotating down toward the ground. Dwapek screamed as he flew through the air, the heavy links of the chain falling all around him.

He landed on his side, a portion of the iron sitting heavily upon his left leg. He groaned as he struggled to pull free of the weight. A deafening bellowed erupted from the monster before him. *I hope he understands that I just freed him.*

The crowd certainly did. The tone in the arena shifted from anger, to shock, to dread. In a matter of heartbeats, the filled seats closest to the edge of the arena emptied as patrons scrambled to climb out of harm's way.

Maul took one step toward him, then flattened himself so Dwapek could climb back onto his back. Once seated, Dwapek impressed upon Maul's mind the idea of climbing out of the arena. The bear roared and started forward at a trot.

Maul picked up speed and Dwapek hoped he was right about the bear's ability to jump. Otherwise his wild plan would end in disaster before it began.

The distance Maul traveled on each four-pawed gallop was astounding. Dwapek watched in awe as the barrier before him drew near; twenty paces, fifteen paces, ten, five, and suddenly they were flying. Dwapek closed his eyes as Maul leaped from the ground toward the balcony above the stone enclosure. He imagined the bear striking the wall hard before falling backward to crush him.

Instead, the bear landed and continued to climb up the seats.

The din of shouts and cries intensified as the reality of Maul's escape became obvious. *A lot less amusing when the bear is after you, isn't it?*

Dwapek spotted the Sachems in their box to his right pointing furiously at the eight guards in charge of keeping the peace, but they were there to break up gambling disputes between Renziks, not to stop a silvertip bear large enough to swallow their heads whole. Still, four of them were equipped with spears, and with Sachem Freedek threatening their lives, all four turned and launched their spears at the bear.

With one hand clinging to the collar, Dwapek sent what little energy he dared to push the first two spears off course. Unfortunately, he was not swift enough to redirect the others. One fell short of its mark, but the other slammed into the bear just below the shoulder.

TO WIELD A PLAGUE

Maul let out a roar of pain as he whirled to face the source of the pain. Dwapek nearly fell from his perch. Maul sat like a wolf, using his hind leg to try to dislodge the spear. His inability to do so only angered him further.

After reestablishing his seated position on Maul's neck, Dwapek noted something worse than the spear in the bear's shoulder. He could feel Sachem Grinnald drawing in power. He too was a wielder adept and surely more skilled than Dwapek.

"Maul, we need to leave. Turn around and leave."

Maul either didn't comprehend or was too enraged to listen. Instead, he growled in the general direction from which the spear had come and charged forward, bounding along the perimeter of the arena toward both the guards and the Sachems. Concerned about the wound, Dwapek leaned over to look and saw the spear lodged into flesh but little blood. Unlike Maul's mood, his movement was wholly unaffected.

Dwapek extended his consciousness toward the bear once more, but was met by an impassable wall of rage and pain.

Sachem Grinnald continued to draw power as they approached.

The spear lodged below Maul's shoulder was just within reach as Dwapek stretched one hand down to grasp it. He pulled but it didn't budge. Again. Nothing.

I'm going to die, but I'm not going to go down without first doing something very stupid. Dwapek released his grip on the metal collar and swung his legs down so his feet were on either side of the spear. Then, gripping it tight in both hands, he pushed off with his feet. The spear pulled free and Dwapek fell off to the side, nearly trampled by Maul's hind paws. He landed on his back, on the wooden seating, but his momentum caused him to roll off and land facedown on the floor between this and the row below. It hurt, but not so much as the death he had coming, should he not escape with Maul, which at this point did not look promising.

Scrambling to his feet, spear in hand, Dwapek looked on helplessly as Sachem Grinnald sent a blast of power straight for Maul. Unlike Dwapek's own magical attempts, this one hit the bear square in the face, knocking his head to the side before he suddenly collapsed.

Dwapek's stomach lurched. *No!* The silvertip remained where he was, motionless. A wave of despair rolled over Dwapek like the inevitability of death that awaited him if he was captured. *When* he was captured. *Come on. Get up!*

The patrons who had cleared the way for the bear continued to back away from Dwapek. But Sachem Freedek shouted to the remaining guards, four of whom held swords. Pointing to Dwapek only a dozen paces away, he yelled, "Seize him!"

Not good.

He did have a spear, and perhaps some ability to wield magic, but how much, he had no idea. The Renzik guards approached with caution, giving Dwapek time to prepare. He sent his mind into the stone below, but felt an ache in his bones the likes of which he'd not felt since the first time he'd wielded power. He had reached his limit. His body was warning him that his bones were at their breaking point.

Dwapek saw Maul's head rise. *He's not dead.* Sachem Grinnald noticed as well, turning his attention back to the bear. Another blow to the head would surely be fatal. Maul staggered back up to all fours, still dazed as Sachem Grinnald prepared to put an end to him. Dwapek took a step further, hefted his spear, then threw with all his might. He didn't dare use magic to strengthen the throw, but it sailed through the air in a perfect line before slamming deep into Sachem Grinnald's side just below the ribs. The wielder adept stumbled back a few steps before turning slowly to regard his assailant, eyes wide with the shock of betrayal. He opened his mouth to say something, but his words were garbled by an outpouring of blood. He fell onto his face.

Sachem Freedek bellowed, "You've sealed your fate, boy!"

"You and Petregof already did that."

Dwapek's gaze drifted over to his father, who glared with bristling eyes. Dwapek could guess his thoughts. *My son, the traitor. Should have killed him myself back on the Veld.*

Then Maul threw his head forward and roared a warning. All the Sachems cowered under the weight of the vociferous cry.

Dwapek was not among them. He was distracted by the host of Renziks he saw approaching from behind the bear. Each of them carried a long spear.

Dwapek yelled. "Maul, run!"

The bear ignored him, releasing another powerful roar before bounding toward the Sachems who had begun to scatter. Sachem Lephrem was too slow. Maul's front right paw swung like a spiked club, sending the comparatively diminutive Renzik soaring through the air to land like a sack of abandoned tart berries.

Meanwhile, the spears drew nearer.

"Maul, you have to run!"

This time the bear at least acknowledged Dwapek, but quickly turned back to seek vengeance against those he believed responsible for the spear to his shoulder. He pounced on another Renzik, Dwapek wasn't sure who, but he was glad for the cacophony of other sounds that blocked out the tearing of flesh and bone as Maul put his name to use.

I need to do something. Dwapek pulled out the stone once more, praying that some of its residual energy had returned. When he drew in, he was once again . . . pleasantly surprised by how quickly it had restored much of its base energy. In an effort to protect his bones, Dwapek drove his mind to the energy beneath his feet. Holding the stone in hand while drawing power from elsewhere would protect him against fatal bone degradation, much more so than drawing from the bedrock below directly. Dwapek drew in more energy from his surroundings.

Poised to push his mind toward Maul's, he hesitated. This would be his last chance, he knew. It needed to be—

The spear-wielding Renziks were easily within range. It needed to be now. Conjuring his best image of a dead bear, dozens of spears protruding from its fur, he sent it toward the mind of the bear with as much will as he could muster.

Maul was preparing to crush another fleeing Sachem beneath the weight of his monstrous paws, but he stopped midstride and turned. Seeing the approaching guards, at least two dozen of them, Maul growled, then crouched to launch himself into the fray.

Dwapek shouted, "Maul! You need to run!" But bears did not speak Renzik. Dwapek needed something else, something more. He sent another image, the same image he sent before, the one of a mother bear with her cubs. Then he visualized Maul running free along the small stream Dwapek had crossed upon first entering the Valley of Nar. With as much mental fortitude as he could muster, he slammed the weight of these images into the wall of will that had thus far kept him at arm's length from the bear's mind.

This was no different. Maul lunged for the oncoming Renzik guards. Then he reached down with his mouth and took the corpse of Sachem Lephrem in his flesh-tearing teeth and whipped his head back then forward, flinging the body of the dead Sachem right into the guards. The first few were able to dive out of harm's way, but those standing behind were not so lucky. Blood trailed the corpse as it flew through the air, a gruesome scene for even a battle-hardened Renzik. Dwapek coughed on his own vomit and averted his eyes.

The ground thundered and he looked up from where vomit pooled at his feet. *Earthmother, save me!* Maul was bounding straight for him. *Apparently he didn't appreciate the warning.*

Shouts rang out from the guards and several threw their spears. One overshot its target, and would have taken Dwapek in the chest if he hadn't rolled to the side. Another thudded beside him. *Are they aiming at Maul or me?* He rose to his feet, ready to jump out of the way of the oncoming behemoth. Maul corrected his path, which meant he was still heading straight for Dwapek. Sachem Grinnald's magical shot to the head seemed to have been effective. Then again, being flattened by a bear would be better than the traitor's death he'd surely receive at the hands of Sachem Freedek.

He closed his eyes and braced himself, as ready as anyone could be when expecting to be crushed to death. *Please, death by paw, not teeth. Paw not teeth. Paw not teeth. Paw not . . .*

Maul stopped moving right in front of Dwapek. He could feel the vile breath, the scent of blood from the bear's recent kill mixing with the rotting flesh of whatever else he was fed. From what Dwapek knew of such things, it had probably been days since the bear had eaten. Just like people, animals tended to be meaner when hungry.

Dwapek opened his eyes in time to see Maul lower his head and shoulders. What's more, Dwapek felt a mental connection to the creature. It wasn't like with a rabbit, or the deer. The bear was not giving over control. But Dwapek sensed the invitation, a sort of kinship. Another spear bounced off the wooden bench to Dwapek's right. *Time to go.*

Dwapek grabbed a spear from the ground beside him, then clambered up the neck of the beast, wincing as he saw two other spears implanted in Maul's back. Once Dwapek was up, Maul returned to all fours, the action knocking one of the spears free. *Good, must not have been too deep.*

Still, half the guards held their weapons upright as they ran to intercept. Dwapek pushed as simple a message as he could to Maul. "Go!"

Either Maul understood the intent of the words or he recognized the danger. In any case, he raced up the remaining benches toward the open plaza within which the arena was situated.

As they ascended the tiered seating to ground level, Dwapek saw that the crowd had mostly receded into the outskirts of the main plaza surrounding the Crixus. This was one of the widest sections of the chasm. Aside from the newly arrived guards and the Sachems, who apparently believed they'd somehow be protected, everyone else hid. Heads poked out from behind carts, wagons, or the more permanent fixtures along the edges of the gorge to witness the outcome of the gripping scene that had befallen the Crixus.

A spear flew by Dwapek's head, just missing Maul's own. There were still close to a dozen spears remaining. Holding on with one hand, he turned to meet the threat. He did so in time to bat aside an incoming projectile with his spear. This worked, but between the lumbering motion of the bear's stride and the one-handed defense, Dwapek slipped from his perch on Maul's shoulders, though he remained atop the bear.

Pain shot down the length of his arm, his shoulder felt like it might have separated, but he managed to hold on. Bursts of heat flared at each bounce of the bear's gallop. This forced him to release the spear in his hand in exchange for a handful of brown fur. Recognizing Dwapek's plight, Maul slowed to a stop, allowing Dwapek to pull himself up.

Then Maul turned on his hind legs, towering over the plaza like a monolith of legendary power. He raised his massive paws above his head and roared in the direction of the guards. The sound was visceral, the fiercest yet. The cry was wet with rage, vengeance, and hurt, and it shook everything within the chasm.

Fearing this meant the beast would attack once again, Dwapek pleaded, "Maul, we *need* to go."

Much to Dwapek's surprise, the bear growled but relented. He turned just in time to avoid a projectile that would have hit him in the neck. Instead, the shaft struck at an off angle, glancing harmlessly off Maul's thick hide. As they resumed their flight, Dwapek knew the rest of the spears would be on their way. Unfortunately, this time he was powerless to do anything about it. He turned to watch in horror as two of the remaining spears headed straight for them.

All he could do was observe as both spears planted themselves in Maul's hide. The sudden shock caused Maul to stumble and Dwapek held on for dear life as the bear attempted to regain his footing. *Please, please, please, be all right.*

Maul fell forward but didn't roll to the side, thankfully. Dwapek remained seated, praise the Earthmother, but this creature had been his only chance to escape the chasm and it was lying down on the ground like a glutton after a feast, vulnerable should any other Renziks take up spears.

The beast groaned, and Dwapek's heart fluttered as Maul slowly rose onto all fours. His moan reminded Dwapek of Big Paw, the sound of resigned defeat. The creature extended his right hind leg and shook it, then repeated the same with the others before shaking his rear end. The spear on his left fell to the ground, while the other two remained. Maul released another deafening roar, then took off again at a gallop. *Thank you!*

Shouts rang out as those who had hoped the bear was finished saw their dream disappear.

The gap in the chasm narrowed then turned up ahead.

Sachem Freedek's voice rang out above the rest. "This isn't over! Traitor! You're more forsaken than those who sent you! You'll never be safe."

Dwapek didn't so much as turn to regard the source of the voice. He sank down in his seat, still shaking with tension as Maul carried him away from immediate danger. For all Dwapek knew, Maul would eat him the moment they were free of this place. But that was okay. That would be better than whatever Freedek would have done to him if he was captured. All things considered, this was the best day he'd had since leaving for the hunt.

Chapter 12

Bright spears of sunlight shot through a small break in the angry storm clouds to the north in a brilliant display of the Earthmother's beauty. The dual nature of the goddess was perfectly reflected in the contrasting life-giving light amid the approaching storm. Tiny flecks of snow shone like stars in a black sky. Dwapek shivered against the cold bite of the wind as evening approached.

Maul continued to move at a lope, though he had slowed considerably, and there seemed to be a wobble in his gait. They traveled north toward the Valley of Nar. The bear had still not allowed Dwapek into his mind, but the hitch in his step told the story of his injury. The creature would certainly need the spears removed once they reached the safety of the Valley.

Dwapek dared not climb back to investigate the damage done by the shafts in Maul's hind, not while

Maul was moving. And they couldn't afford to stop moving. Instead, he endeavored to drive his mind's eye directly into the flesh to assess and heal if necessary. He had the confidence from having healed a far more grievous wound. The question now was how much more magic he could wield before surpassing his limits. Using his sense of the world's energy, he took hold of just a sliver. It would be days before his bones returned to full strength. However, he also suspected the stone's density had been at least partially restored. This would offset the degradation to his bones so long as he only used a small amount.

Dwapek had little difficulty locating the afflicted areas on the bear's hind, one of which appeared to be relatively superficial. Dwapek moved from there and focused his attention on the deeper spear, which was tearing the bear's flesh as it bounced with every step. That needed to be addressed—now.

The painful ache deep in his bones screamed caution, but this was necessary for both of them. Dwapek pushed as much energy as he dared. The blue stone glowed, illuminating the area around him. The fast-falling snowflakes still limited visibility, but he was able to make out the hulking shape of Maul, a moving mountain of muscle, fur, and determination. The area mended, pushing the metal tip of the spear away from the worst of the damage. It wasn't enough to fully dislodge it, but the inflammation diminished and Maul's pace soon increased. Dwapek released his hold on the

Earthmother's power and sank into his seat. He had expended far more than was safe. At this point, he was certain a simple fall would be his undoing.

Aside from this, Dwapek had no idea what he would do moving forward. He was completely alone, hunted by the Renzik, and as soon as Petregof learned of what had taken place, the Forsaken would hunt him as well.

He shook his head. *Have to stay alive today before I worry about tomorrow.*

This portion of the Veld nearest the sea was the thinnest, which meant they descended from the plateau into the Valley just before the sun disappeared behind the horizon. Maul stopped at a stream to drink, and Dwapek hopped down, the insides of his legs aching despite the thick fur padding. He drank deeply from the ice-cold water coming down from the snowy peaks beyond. He took in water until he thought his stomach might burst, then drank a little more. It felt good to have *something*, anything, in his stomach after going the entire day without a meal. He had no idea when he might have his next. But at least he would have a spear for hunting as soon as it was light. He just had to manage pulling it out of Maul without being eaten.

He still wasn't completely certain Maul wouldn't eat him either way, though the bear had shown no aggression since their departure. *Time to find out.*

Maul was still drinking as Dwapek walked over to where the weapon hung down. He started at the neck and patted the creature. "Maul, I need to remove these spears from your flesh."

Dwapek worked his way to the bear's hindquarters, and took hold of the nearest spear. The bear stiffened and growled. His huge, blocky head turned, water dripping from his mouth. Dwapek could imagine his blood dripping from Maul's mouth. He blinked away the image, but the concern remained. The bear had slain hundreds of Renziks already. What was one more?

Dwapek let out a heavy breath. *This needs to be done.* "I'm going to pull this out of your hind. Is that okay?"

The beast glared but made no move to stop him, or to eat him, which he figured was a good sign. Dwapek readjusted his grip, and another growl nearly caused him to abandon the idea entirely. *Be strong. He needs this spear removed; he deserves that much, regardless of your own fate.*

"All right, Maul, I'm going to pull on the count of three."

"One." *Please don't eat me.*
"Two." *Please don't eat me.*
"Three." *Please don't eat!*

Nothing happened. *I'm still alive . . . oh . . . right . . .* He was supposed to pull the spear out.

He yanked as hard as he could and was rewarded with a hard fall backward as the spear pulled free. Maul roared and whipped around to face Dwapek's fallen form. Teeth the size of his fingers flashed and he knew this was it, the end of the dance with death he'd thus far managed to prolong. *Play with sharp things enough and eventually you get cut*, he recalled his father saying. Not that any of this had been a conscious effort on his part. He was just trying to survive.

Much to Dwapek's shock, instead of swallowing his head whole, the bear released a heavy puff of putrid breath, then shook his body as if trying to vacate the accumulating snow on his fur. Then he sat on his hind end like a wolf, and pulled himself forward. *Scratching himself?* "Does this mean you're not going to eat me?"

The bear snorted, then pushed past him. "Hey, stop. I need to look at the wound to make sure the bleeding isn't too severe. Then I'll need to pull out the other one."

The bear paused. Dwapek didn't know if the creature fully understood what he had said, but he allowed Dwapek to inspect the wound. The bleeding was minimal since he'd mended the worst of it previously. He would mend it further in the morning, if he survived until then.

The second spear came out more easily and with less of a reaction from Maul, who started trudging north once again. Dwapek left the first spear where it was while hefting the second. *I only need one.* Then he followed after Maul.

"Hey, wait for me."

Maul stopped at a sloped, snow-covered area of earth and began clawing feverishly. "What's the plan here?"

Dwapek watched in perplexed awe as half of Maul's massive body disappeared into the hillside, though part of the trick was due to the renewed vigor of the snowfall.

Holding on to his spear, Dwapek crept over toward Maul. As he drew near, he decided to set the spear somewhere he'd be able to find later and pushed it into the ground. "Stay here." He paused for a moment to consider the lunacy of having just made demands of an inanimate object, then decided this was one of the most normal things he had done in days.

He scanned the area. *Where did you go?* He'd lost track of Maul and the snow was so thick he couldn't see further than his own hand before him. He felt around with each step, his face accosted by thick flakes, until . . . *ugh*. He was stopped by a wall of muscle, fat, and wet fur.

Before he had a chance to consider what part of the bear he'd just waylaid, a rumbling growl sounded. It reminded him that the unspoken covenant he and Maul had forged as a means to escape was a fragile thing without an agreed-upon end date. He may have already overstayed his welcome.

His reflexive response was, "Sorry." Followed by a step backward, eyes downcast, hands raised in the least threatening way he knew. Between the darkness and the snow, he couldn't see a thing, but he held the pose nonetheless.

He could see the shifting of shadows, but couldn't make out more than that, given the visibility. He slid a hand into the pocket with the stone, but quickly abandoned the idea of using it even to the smallest degree.

"Maul?"

His coat suddenly tightened, pulled from behind until he was lifted into the air. "Maul? What are you—?"

His legs kicked and his arms flailed, but it was as futile as a toddler resisting the will of a parent carrying them to the tent for bedtime. He relented and felt the bobbing of Maul's steps, relaxing after a few moments as he recognized Maul was not chewing on his flesh.

Maul set him down and he stumbled back into—a wall? Feeling around with his hands, he recognized a rough, rounded space and his hands came back with a bit of loose soil and stone. There was also a distinct lack of snowfall overhead. Dwapek could make out the faintest light of an opening. The cave wasn't deep and he took a few steps until he felt the cold wetness of snow brushing against his face.

"Did you really just dig yourself a cave?"

The bear grunted then the beast's enormous forehead was nudging him backward, into the hole once more. "Hey, watch it! What are you doing?" He attempted to maneuver his way back out from the opening, but Maul adjusted and simply pushed him further in. A low rumble escaped his throat, but it wasn't an angry warning. At least, Dwapek hoped it wasn't. It seemed more like an elder telling a child to stop squirming while they applied a salve to a cut.

A hard knock from Maul's nose and Dwapek fell backward into the freshly dug hole. The cavity went down at a slight angle, but not far. For freshly dug earth, the landing was not as soft as one might expect. Still, a sharp pain in his side had him worried his ribs had grown brittle enough to crack, but it subsided, and he took a pain-free breath. *Praise the Earthmother.*

To his surprise, Maul did not molest him further. Instead, he lay down just close enough to the edge of the small opening for Dwapek to remain where he was without feeling like he might suffocate. The bear settled in and released another deep rumble that Dwapek decided was more akin to a sigh than anything else.

Maul repositioned himself once, then twice, attempting to settle into a comfortable position for rest. Understanding dawned on Dwapek. Understanding, and a feeling of utter mental inferiority for not understanding sooner. "You're keeping me from freezing to death in the storm, aren't you?"

Maul didn't respond, but the slow, easy breaths of a creature on the verge of slumber were enough of an answer. Dwapek lay between the earthen wall and the bear and felt the warmth in the space already growing comfortable. He allowed a sigh of his own, feeling more at peace than he had since before leaving on the hunt. He might be hungry, tired, without anywhere to go, and likely to be hunted relentlessly until the end of his days, but in this moment, he was safe, warm, and without a single immediate threat. He slid his hand into his pocket, feeling the smooth stone, and closed his eyes. Sleep stole all other thoughts.

Chapter 13

Even tucked away as Dwapek was within the hastily dug alcove, the light of day had no problem forcing its way in to wake him. Maul, on the other hand, remained unaffected, his slow, rhythmic breathing proof that the bear still slumbered. Who could blame the beast? Aside from the fight within and without the arena, he'd run for hours after having been struck with spears and magic alike, all while carrying a Renzik on his back.

Still, Dwapek's own reluctance to rise was challenged by his concern that if they didn't keep moving, they would be found and killed. The snowstorm had likely forced whatever expeditionary force had been sent after them to shelter, but the search would have resumed by now and he and Maul needed to do the same.

Standing, Dwapek could see enough of the outside to confirm they'd received no small amount of snow. Enough to nearly cover the opening of their cave.

He smiled widely. Any tracks would have been completely covered by the snow. And based on the dark-gray cloud cover, more was on its way. It had been a while since the Earthmother had shown him this kind of compassion, though he figured he was owed some luck after the last few weeks of disaster. He prayed the Earthmother agreed.

Dwapek's bones still ached from the usage of so much magic the day before, but it was a distant, dull ache, not the acute sense that the slightest mishap would be his undoing. Feeling this, he resolved to finish healing what remained of Maul's injuries. The stone's residual energy had been fully restored so the effect on Dwapek's bones should be minimal. As such, he was able to heal each puncture. By the time he finished, Maul had stirred.

Whether the bear understood what Dwapek had just done or not was unknowable, but Maul seemed in good spirits. Once out of the makeshift cave, he lowered himself down for Dwapek to climb onto.

"I could get used to this," remarked the battered but recovering Renzik as he moved further into the Valley of Nar atop a silvertip bear.

Dwapek was all the more grateful as the snow returned. The issue now was that the same snow that was preventing them from being tracked also prevented them from foraging or hunting. Part of Dwapek's mind, the perpetually paranoid part, still wondered if Maul might simply be keeping him alive in case he needed a snack later. He didn't know much about the eating habits of bears, but he knew for certain that *he* was *very* hungry. Maul stopped by a stream for water, so Dwapek drank, but it did little to quell his hunger.

"Ow!" yelped Dwapek as something wet and heavy slammed into his face. "What in the—"

Looking at his feet, he saw a fish the length of his arm still flopping on the ground, bloody streaks left from Maul's teeth. Dwapek looked at the bear, who stood in the middle of the narrow river up to his elbows—or would it be knees with a bear? He wasn't sure. One thing about which he was confident, however, was that if bears could grin, he was doing so now, another massive fish in his maw.

"Proud of yourself, are you?"

Maul chomped a few times, then swallowed his catch whole. He turned away from Dwapek, his attention returning to the water, and Dwapek decided it would be nice to eat some fish, raw or not.

As the sun disappeared beyond the nearby peaks, a new wave of intense snow settled upon their path, forcing them to seek shelter. So far as Dwapek could tell, they had traveled north across the narrowest portion of the Veld and the Valley of Nar and were now entering the foothills marking the southern edges of the White Reaches.

Dwapek's main concern was that Maul might misstep as he negotiated the ever-increasing slopes, some of which included ominous steep drop-offs into unknown depths, given the visibility issue.

He breathed a sigh of relief when the barrage of snow suddenly ended beneath the cover of an overhang of stone. Looking about, Dwapek was further relieved to see that this led to an opening in the stone easily large enough for both himself and Maul to fit inside. In fact, as he peered in, he realized this was actually a cave. Swinging his legs on the left side of the bear, Dwapek slid to the stone floor.

He walked toward the dark opening ahead of Maul, glad to be out of the wind. He noticed a few marks in the light snow but didn't recognize them, and the snow disappeared altogether as he approached the opening.

He heard a snort from Maul and turned to see that the bear had stopped several paces back.

"What's your problem? This is exactly what we need right now. Don't tell me you want to waste your energy digging your own hole when we have a perfectly good one right here."

Dwapek continued on, passing the threshold into an opening large enough for two silvertips to walk abreast. That thought gave him pause. Could this be the home of another bear? Worse, a family of bears? Did Maul somehow know this?

Suddenly the scent of something foul wafted into Dwapek's nose. He gagged.

"Ugh. What is that smell?" It was putrid, like compost gone very wrong. A growl sounded from behind and Dwapek turned slowly, speaking as he did. "You can't scare away a bad smell with your . . ."

Dwapek saw the cause of Maul's aggression—sort of. A dark shape, larger than Maul, approached from beyond the rock overhang at the entrance to the cave. Whatever it was, it was big.

Maul's growl became more fervent, more agitated as he backed his way deeper into the cave, toward Dwapek.

The shape emerged from the cover of the snow and Dwapek gasped. An arachnid rivaling Maul for size crept forward like a thief ready to pilfer something right from under someone's nose. "Nazca," cursed Dwapek.

Gripping his spear tighter, Dwapek felt powerless. He'd seen more than a dozen Renziks battle a single Nazca to no avail. He very much doubted he and his spear, or even Maul with all his might, could stand against the approaching spider. He had the stone, but he questioned whether it would be enough even if he was fully recovered.

"We should go," whispered Dwapek to Maul, who was now beside him. The bear continued to growl. Dwapek drew in power from his surroundings, then reached into his pocket to grip the artifact to preserve his bones. "We need to go—now." Dwapek pulled out the stone and sent the mental idea of them traveling into the cave, hoping that might better convey his

TO WIELD A PLAGUE

point to the bear. The stone glowed a faint blue before he slid it into his pocket. To Dwapek's surprise, Maul lowered his front end for Dwapek to climb. He did, holding his spear on his right hand, not that it would do him much good.

Once Dwapek was secure, Maul lunged forward toward the approaching Nazca and roared. The arachnid paused. *That's something*, thought Dwapek.

Then Maul turned and lumbered into the blackness of the cave. Dwapek hadn't the slightest idea how the creature avoided walls, but perhaps the time these things spent in caves gave them better night vision than Renziks.

The stench of decay grew stronger as they descended into the depths of the cave. Dwapek just prayed there was another way out. If they needed to fight the thing, it might have been better to do so out where he could see.

Maul suddenly stopped, causing Dwapek to nearly fall forward from his position behind the bear's neck. Perhaps it was the slight movement of air, or the empty sound of Maul's labored breathing, but Dwapek had the distinct feeling that they had entered a vast space. He saw nothing but dark. Maul growled low once again, and Dwapek heard a faint clicking. At first it was just a few light clicks, the sound of stone striking stone, though not hard. It varied in volume, giving further validity to his theory that they were standing within a large, open cavern. Feathers of fear tickled every hair on Dwapek's body. He had a strong suspicion as to the source of these sounds but was loath to admit to himself that it was so.

Maul backed up ever so slowly, growling all the while.

Dwapek pulled in energy from around him and withdrew the stone. It illuminated the space with a blue glow. The ceiling rose from the wall at an angle before disappearing completely into a blackness so resolute the blue light could not pierce it. Looking about the rest of the space, at least that which was made visible by the stone's faint light, gave Dwapek the kind of chills that brought even the bravest of warriors to their knees with trembling.

The shiny armored legs, heads, and bodies of dozens of Nazca reflected the blue light like stars in a clear sky. No, not stars. Meteors.

And this was not a cave. It was a colony.

Chapter 14

THE CREATURES CIRCLED SLOWLY AS if they were all of one mind, though their movements were not identical. "We should not have come down here," whispered Dwapek in a weak, cracked voice.

Clicking echoed down the corridor from which they had entered. The Nazca that had pursued them into this place had caught up to them. Maul shuffled out of the way of the opening, not that he or Dwapek wished to be any closer to the other predators in the chamber.

The Nazca reached the mouth of the tunnel, then stopped.

Is it too much to ask that the thing might leave the tunnel open for us to escape?

Looking around, Dwapek noticed that all of the arachnids had stopped approaching. Not a single Nazca moved. "What are they doing?"

Maul didn't respond, but his growling grew more feral, or was that fearful? He wasn't fully attuned to recognizing what he sensed through their mental connection.

A faint light appeared from within another tunnel at least fifty paces across the cavern. White light blossomed brighter, moving eerily down the large tunnel into the cavern.

"We should *not* have come down here," Dwapek said as a creature of utter horror emerged.

This Nazca, if it could even be called that, towered over all others in the space. Light emanated from its massive abdomen, which was the size of one of the motionless Nazca beside it. *How is that thing doing this? Actually, how is that thing a thing at all?* It was from a nightmare the likes of which he had not the imagination to conjure.

The light wasn't blinding, but it was enough to illuminate the extent of the chamber, and everything within it. Giant crystals of all colors drank in the light, a cache in the ceiling large enough to enrich the tribes for generations, if someone could somehow rid this place of an army of Nazca and extract even half of it. If the circumstances had been different, this cave could have been beautiful. Filled as it was with giant arachnids, it was a place of horror.

Even Maul's low rumbling growl shifted from an angry warning to something closer to a fearful whine.

The enormous glowing creature crept toward Dwapek and the bear with disquieting grace, gliding forward like an inevitable wave pushing its way toward shore to drown any who dared stand too close.

Dwapek regretting having climbed down from Maul's back. He stood with his back against the wall beside a bear that had recently attempted to tear him apart limb from limb. That seemed like a far better end than whatever this monster before him might do. He wanted to run, but there was nowhere to go, and the effort, he knew, would be futile. This was it. This was his end. His hand still held to the blue stone, though all the magic flowing through it had dissipated.

He gritted his teeth, despair turning to anger. *If I'm to die, I'm gonna take this big one with me.* He laughed at the absurdity of the idea. *I couldn't even take down a bear with the stone.* Though it might be nice to go down trying.

The glowing creature stopped just five paces before him and he stared into its four black eyes, two of which glinted around the edges. The centermost were larger, ringed by a red-orange glow with a center blacker than the absence of light itself. The depths of shadow appeared palpable, as if dark hands might suddenly extend from within them to swallow anything or anyone who dared offer light.

He wanted to draw in power, to go down swinging, but he was just *so* tired. Terrified to his core, and utterly exhausted. If he had been capable of fighting before, the eyes of this creature had extinguished his ability once and for all. There was an intelligence in the way it moved, in the way the other arachnids cowered at its mere presence. If evil could manifest itself within the world, this was it.

The spider crept forward once more, close enough that when it lifted the nearest leg and extended it forward, Dwapek saw that it would be able to touch him. He felt a new wave of cold terror as the sharp, shiny spear that was its leg came within a handsbreadth of his shoulder.

Dwapek was unable to take his eyes off the spider before him. Then, out of the corner of his eye, he saw another black spear move, this one toward the bear. Maul's perpetual growl intensified.

Another black sinewy leg extended toward Dwapek, this one coming to rest just above his other shoulder. He was trembling as both suddenly dropped to put pressure on each of his shoulders, pulling him forward. His shaky legs moved of their own accord, Dwapek's will to resist having disappeared into the pools of the black abyss.

Before he knew it, he stood directly below the mouth of the creature, its teeth, sharp like flakes of obsidian, glinting as they dripped a white liquid to the ground at Dwapek's feet. It reeked of sulfur.

The back corner of his mind wished to flee, but the slight pressure from the two legs pressing from behind his shoulders was all it took to quell thoughts of resistance.

Maul had stopped growling, apparently resigned to whatever fate he and Dwapek would meet.

Dwapek stared up as the spider's mouth opened, revealing more rows of shiny, yellow, swordlike teeth. He would be swallowed whole if the spider wished it. He hoped for a quick, crushing bite first, and shuddered at the thought.

His voice was but a light, cracked whisper as he said, "Please . . ."

Then another sound echoed in from somewhere to Dwapek's right. It seemed to come from the tunnel through which he and Maul had entered. At first, he fancied it part of his imagination, but as it grew louder, Dwapek saw the mouth of the spider retract, its body pivoting to face the source of the distraction.

Dwapek turned his head and saw an orange glow leak in from the corridor.

A high-pitched, raspy exclamation made its way into the chamber. "He ought to suffer long and hard for dragging us through that damned blizzard into this place of deathly rot. The stench is unbearable!"

A deeper voice responded, "Is that supposed to be some sick joke?"

"Oh, hah!" said another before being cut off by a third.

"No way! He's not clever enough for that sort of wit."

"Silence! All of you." Dwapek recognized the voice of Sachem Freedek. He continued, "If this is the home of that silvertip, there might be more of them. You would do well to shut your mouths and prepare yourselves for batt—"

His words cut off as he and several members of his group stepped into the vast cavern.

"What in the deathly fires of . . ." His voice rang with both fear and awe. His gaze finally met Dwapek's, and his eyes widened further. "What dark evil have you awakened?"

Dwapek opened his mouth but his words were like smoke. What was there to say? They would all be dead soon, anyhow. He didn't need to defend his name or his actions. Not to a traitor like Freedek.

Moving his torch back and forth like a spear, Freedek said, "Back up the tunnel."

Before Freedek had managed more than a couple steps, shouts echoed from deeper within. The cries of death chased out a party of at least twenty Renziks. *There must be connecting side tunnels.* It had been dark as Maul carried Dwapek down so he hadn't noticed. A meaningless observation now that they were all moments away from death.

Dwapek counted five torches and the glint of steel from a few swords. The rest wielded long spears designed to combat larger creatures like bears. A cave filled with Nazca, however, was not something even the most paranoid Renzik planned for. This was like standing at the foot of a mountain at the onset of a great avalanche while waving a shovel. Judging by the horror on the faces of those who had emerged from the corridor, they would have welcomed an avalanche if given the choice.

Blood glistened off the black-carapaced legs of the Nazca that had forced the party out of the tunnel, the torches illuminating the life essence of their comrades.

Eyes fixed on the newcomers, Dwapek didn't see the black leg move until it was pushing him aside. There was no violence in the motion, more like a parent absentmindedly brushing a child out of the way as they moved to complete one task or another.

Apparently I'm dessert.

He wasn't so sure he liked the idea of having to watch as his brethren, enemies or not, were mutilated by this nightmare and its . . . children? Yes, of course. This had to be the queen. Could this be the hive Petregof mentioned? If the stories were true, this was the place where all the Nazca of the north lived, and before him was *the* queen Nazca, the matriarch of desolation.

The pack of soldiers formed an ever-tighter circle of defense as the queen moved closer. The other Nazca formed up around them as well, but they maintained a perimeter of about ten paces with an opening through which death itself approached.

Sachem Freedek stepped forward and raised his torch like a sword in an attempt to ward off the Nazca. Dwapek watched in dismay as the monstrous creature used one of its black spear-like legs to strike the torch out of Sachem Freedek's hands. It crashed into the wall behind the group, its light flickering sadly in the gloom. The action had been so forceful it caused Freedek to fall to the side. He was quick to recover, drawing his blade before retreating slowly back to the false safety of the group.

Then the queen shot forth one of her legs and stabbed through the spear-wielding Renzik beside Freedek. He was lifted high into the air, screaming all the while, before being whipped to the side. The action caused him to slide off her leg, landing in the middle of three Nazca who suddenly rushed to tear apart the body, consuming it piece by piece.

Dwapek turned away from the sight. Meanwhile, he felt the tingle of magic growing both from within the group of Renziks and the Nazca. The latter was far greater. The queen must have sensed her enemies wielding.

Dwapek looked around the cavern filled with Nazca, presumably most of the hive, including the queen, and reached into his pocket. He still held the blue stone in one hand, though he channeled no magic at the moment. But his other hand clasped the bone necklace, the Etzem Tzaraath. He pulled it forth and stared at it in the white light of the queen Nazca.

Why this hadn't occurred to him sooner, he had no idea, but that was no matter. The idea was here now. *If I'm to die, I may as well do something noble.*

The fearful, self-loathing voice in the back of his mind reminded him that no one would know that it had been him. That his sacrifice would be the reason they were free to roam the Valley without fear of the Nazca.

It doesn't matter. I'll know. And if Targon was wrong, or a figment of my imagination, I'll at least die in the pursuit of something noble. My father would be proud, if he knew.

That would be enough. It had to be. It was all he had.

Holding the Etzem Tzaraath high above his head, he squeezed his fist around it and drove his mind into the stone around him, preparing to draw as much as his body and mind would permit.

Several blasts of magic shot forth from within the group, all aimed at the queen Nazca, who, for the first time, released a ghastly shriek of rage, the likes of which could have momentarily crippled the bravest of warriors. Then she stomped forward, radiating magic. One sweep of her leg across the assembled Renziks scattered them to the left of the corridor's entrance. Dwapek had no idea what method of communication existed, if any, but the other Nazca seemed to have received the cue to attack because they all moved in unison against the dazed contingent of Renziks, some of whom did not move after being struck with such ferocity.

The queen rounded on Dwapek with incredible agility given her size. But Dwapek knew better than to deny the impossible as she stared him in the face.

He'd lost focus, and therefore his hold on the power residing within the solid rock beneath his feet. *Come on.* He reached once again for the power. Just before unleashing it, he felt another burst of magic from the contingent of Renziks and the queen shrieked once more, the sound grating painfully against his ears. He stumbled back a step, again losing his hold on his magic. Staring at the gaping mouth of the Nazca, teeth dripping with saliva, Dwapek had another idea. Perhaps it was a bad one, but it felt right. *Sometimes the best ideas come to us on a whim without thought or rationale.* His father had told him that years ago when discussing his decision to marry Dwapek's mother. He'd never indicated which type of idea that had been, but Dwapek always liked to think it had been this kind. He hoped so now as well.

He took a short step forward, yelled with all his might, and hurled the Etzem Tzaraath into the still gaping mouth of the Nazca. The creature paused, confused.

Dwapek turned and ran.

"Maul! Let's go!"

He set off toward the entry tunnel. It was unguarded as a result of the killing frenzy set off by the queen. Dwapek ignored the din of battle—no, slaughter. Maul raced toward him but slipped on the slick, blood-covered floor. His body continued its forward momentum, sliding right for Dwapek, who did the only thing he *could* do: jump. By the grace of the gods, he managed to catch fur and pull himself up high enough up to not be flattened by the crushing weight of the bear as it slammed into the cavern wall a moment later. Dwapek clambered up to Maul's shoulders as the bear came back to all fours.

"Go!"

As soon as Dwapek had a good grip on Maul's metal collar, he pulled out his stone. This was the good thing about his situation. He had no more fear. Anything he did now was less risky than doing nothing.

He drew on the latent power stored within the surrounding rock and gem-encrusted walls of the cavern and prepared to wield all of it. The sound of sharp death spikes clanging against the stone floor of the cave from behind confirmed the she-spider's fast approach.

Turning his head to look would be a mistake, but it took all of his will not to do so. If she was in any way enticed to use her magic, and Targon was right about the Etzem Tzaraath, that would be the end of everyone and everything within the cavern and perhaps beyond.

Thus, he focused his attention on the opening just a few paces away, praying it was too small for the queen's bulbous body to navigate. *Come on! Two more strides.*

Motion to his right tipped him off to the fast-approaching form of another Nazca. *No no no!*

He lashed out with the power at his disposal; not directly, however. He had another major task for his magic. But he had to make it into the tunnel. A narrow band of power shot forth into the floor of the cave, sending debris into the path of the Nazca.

As soon as he finished, he slid the stone into his pocket and held on for dear life. If the Nazca had been slowed, it was only slightly. Sharp spear-like legs and body collided with Maul's hind end and Dwapek prepared to be crushed by a falling bear. He readied himself to leap from Maul's back, but instead the bear's body listed and swung to the side. Maul had been midstride at the entrance to the cavern tunnel and the collision did not fully stop his momentum. His hind end slammed into the wall just inside the opening, and a great bellow of pain sounded from the bear. Dwapek's heart fell like a trampled flower. They had come so close. The bear remained unmoving for several heartbeats as their momentum came to an end. Dwapek turned to assess how much longer he had to live. The Nazca had tumbled on past the opening, but the same could not be said of the queen. *Gods above!* She was right there. Her sharp carapaced spear shot forth toward Dwapek and . . .

A deep, earthy moan coincided with a sudden pull forward. Dwapek turned away from the arachnid as he attempted to remain astride the bear. An unbearlike yelp escaped Maul's throat but his forward momentum remained unbroken by the attack.

The response from behind was a sound more chilling than any nightmare could ever hope to be. It was deep-rooted hatred, contempt the likes of which could not be comprehended by the even the most repulsive Renzik—irrational hostility incarnate. If a sound could have weight, this one might have flattened the fleeing Renzik. Maul, however, was a creature capable of carnal fury and continued unaffected.

Maul propelled him along the winding tunnel and Dwapek felt a surge of hope. They were going to escape! Then the staccato clicking and clacking of sharp spikes echoed from behind, impressing an image of the fast-approaching predator.

Dwapek and Maul had been able to outrun the Nazca earlier, but Maul was not at full strength. There was a noticeable hitch in his stride, and the sound of pursuit drew near. Dwapek knew what he needed to do, but would only have the strength to do it once. Without knowing how many other tunnels connected between here and the cave's mouth, he had to wait until they reached the surface . . . *if* they reached the surface.

The way down had seemed much shorter than this. *Come on! Come on!* The sharp footsteps were too close. They weren't going to make it. Not unless he did something right now. Gripping the stone tight, he sent his mind into the ceiling up ahead. With the blue glow of the stone, Dwapek turned to confirm his fears: the icy blue light glistened off the hard exoskeleton of death's pursuit. He could wait no longer.

A spear of light shot forth from ahead as they rounded a corner. *The surface!*

"Come on, Maul!"

The bear let out a grunt of pain. *No! We're so close!* Without further thought, Dwapek channeled just enough power to form a small blade of air and shot it into the black eyes of the Nazca. It shrieked, and their lead increased. But within another three heartbeats, the Nazca had resumed its pursuit. Dwapek prayed he had enough time and strength to survive his next use of power.

The light ahead was so close. This was it. Life or death.

Dwapek drove his mind in the stone ceiling up ahead as he continued past. Then a chilling wave of *something* ripped through him. It was so jarring he lost his grip on Maul, and his magic, as he tumbled to the side just beyond the opening to the cave. He held tight to the artifact, closing his eyes as the blue light flashed blindingly bright. Something momentous had just occurred. It was as indescribable as the changing of a season, and yet he knew a transformation had transpired. He clutched the stone, hand shaking. There was a deep wrongness in the air. A palpable evil.

The Etzem Tzaraath.

Guilt washed through Dwapek, quickly balanced with relief. *They're gone! The Nazca. They're all gone!* He knew this with certainty. Nothing could have withstood such evil . . .

This realization brought about a renewed sense of his own mortality. Dwapek cowered, expecting the plague to take him too, to do its worst. He savored each intake of air, of renewal, ignoring the deep ache of his bones, his injuries, the throbbing in his shoulder, ribs, and leg. He savored each life-giving breath.

The monster that had pursued him from beneath also paused. Dwapek waited, crouching where he was, waiting for the plague to collect its payment. As if in protest, the Nazca before him shrieked and slashed out with one of its front legs.

Dwapek dodged backward, the carapaced spear brushing his beard as it struck air.

Apparently the effects of the queen's death on her hive are not immediate!

He heard Maul growl from behind him. "Get back," Dwapek warned the bear.

With one hand still clutching the blue stone, Dwapek took a step back and extended the stone toward the monster before him. "You should have stayed below with your friends." He sent his mind into the overhanging rock, feeling for existing fault lines while creating others of his own. He could almost taste the paths of crisp, weblike, dormant energy waiting to be used, and this time he didn't hold back. He pulled harder, clung tighter than any Renzik should, for to draw too much matter from an object was to destabilize it. Only this time, that was exactly what he intended.

Dwapek peered into the black eyes of death. *Earthmother, protect me!* He sent a blast of raw power straight into the Nazca. Dwapek groaned as the energy flowed from the stone, through him, and toward the Nazca. The shriek of pain released by the spider was swallowed by the thunder of collapsing rock as Dwapek pulled every last bit of essence from the lines of stone above like a spider pulling the anchors of its web to bring forth its prey.

Dwapek turned away, falling to the earth as shards of stone pelted and cut him where his coat was not thick enough to protect. His lungs burned as they sucked in the dust, and he coughed, then covered his mouth with his sleeve to filter the worst of the debris.

As suddenly as it began, everything grew silent and still. A faint ringing in his ears was all that he could hear as the sun illuminated the slow-moving cloud of thick, gray dust.

Dwapek rose to his feet slowly, cautiously, sharp pain blossoming . . . everywhere. Every joint burned, deep and visceral. This was what he and every other Renzik had been warned against. His bones protested each movement. But there were other, more important things to worry about . . .

Where did Maul go?

"Maul . . . ? Maul . . . ?"

Could a stray boulder have . . .

The dust thinned to reveal a large, thin, dark shape before him, moving up and down. He stepped back nervously as the realization of what it was became apparent; the sharp black leg of a Nazca poked out from within a mound of debris. *How? How is that thing still alive?*

Then another, larger shape grew from the depths of the fading dust cloud accompanied by a loud growl. Teeth flashed. Maul latched on to the leg with his massive jaws and shook his head until the leg pulled free from the rubble, leaving behind the buried body. The bear continued to thrash the leg about, nearly hitting Dwapek before casting it back toward the collapsed tunnel entrance. So far as Dwapek could tell, nothing would be coming through that entrance any time soon. *Good. Very good.*

A sharp voice rang out from behind him, sounding far away. "Hey, what's going on down there? I sensed magic and . . ."

There was a pause before he said, "It's *you*." The tone had changed from genuine concern to anger and fear. "Dwapek the defector."

Dwapek turned slowly to face his accuser. A single Renzik stood sentry, spear in hand just ten paces away.

Dwapek the defector. Is that what they're calling me? Catchy.

He ground his teeth. *But it's a lie.* He had chosen none of this. Well, except perhaps his initial decision to save his mother's life. But what sort of son wouldn't have made that same choice? Everything since then had been a factor of mere survival. He was no traitor. *He* was the victim here.

Dwapek straightened. He had no desire to fight, but he had come too far to walk away in chains.

"No," was all he said as Maul padded over to stand beside him, a low growl of warning echoing throughout the space as he appraised the oncomer.

"No?" responded the Renzik in confusion. He couldn't have been much older than Dwapek. The skin around his eyes was soft and his beard had no gray. Dwapek chuckled to himself. The boy had been left to guard the entrance because he was not trusted to do anything more important.

"No," repeated Dwapek confidently, an edge of finality pressed into the single word. "I don't wish to fight you. Too many have died already." Gesturing with a hand, he continued, "Take whatever equipment you have and return home. The others are gone."

The boy's eyes widened in fear, then narrowed in anger. "You . . . you killed all of them?" He gripped his spear tighter.

Dwapek shook his head. "The Nazca did that well enough on their own. This tunnel leads to a vast chamber, home to hundreds of the monsters. Or, it did." Dwapek indicated with his head to the black leg Maul had just removed from the rubble. "I fled before . . ." *Do I tell him about the Etzem Tzaraath?*

The boy took a few steps closer. "So the Nazca killed everyone. But not you, aye?"

Dwapek knew how crazy it sounded, but it was the truth. *Well, most of the truth.* It would have to be enough.

"You heard the claims about this stone, did you not?"

The boy nodded and took a step closer, resulting in a fresh rumbling growl from Maul.

Dwapek continued. "The remaining Nazca are gone. Every last one of them. Find another tunnel to confirm if you wish, but it is finished."

The boy shook his head. "I . . . I have a duty. I can't just leave you here."

Dwapek scowled and held the stone high, drawing in the smallest trickle of power he dared, just enough for the stone to glow from within the shade cast by the mountainside. "You will leave, or you will perish. That is entirely up to you, but I am leaving the north either way."

Dwapek was not lying. He knew exactly where he was going. He shuffled over toward Maul and climbed onto his back.

"Go home."

Urging the bear forward, he prayed to the Earthmother that he would not be forced to fight. He was certain his bones would crack at the slightest impact. He needed to get as far from this place as possible, but he also needed to rest. Maul was better off, but he too had suffered several injuries, courtesy of the Nazca.

Dwapek kept his eyes trained on the boy as he disappeared out of sight, then let out a long breath of relief. Judging by the wind, and the snow clouds ahead, their tracks would not remain visible for long even if the boy decided to try following at a distance instead of returning home.

Chapter 15

Dwapek leaned forward and hugged Maul's neck, relief filling him with gratitude at what they had just survived. None of it seemed real until he tried moving again and was reminded how much his body had endured. Maul's warmth soaked into him, and it was more than just physical. In spite of the tenuous circumstances of their initial meeting within the arena, they had forged an unshakable bond built from common struggle. Dwapek would be sad to part ways in a few days no matter the necessity. If he remained here in these lands, he would be hunted until the day he was found. He had no doubt Maul would now defend him with his life should the need arrive, and Dwapek could not subject his only friend in the world to such an existence.

So he cherished his remaining time with the bear before going his separate way. He had survived insurmountable odds and learned a great deal about his own abilities and the need to understand his powers more fully. If he was in fact a wielder adept, perhaps he could be allowed to use this power for something good, as intended by the Earthmother.

Much of his time was spent sleeping deeply in shallow caves, burrowed into the warm folds of Maul's thick hide. The bear's sides rose and fell in a slow rhythm, carrying Dwapek off to reflect on all he'd been through over the last few weeks. He returned to the sinkhole with Big Paw. The unspeakable terror of the chase. How the gods had seemed to curse him again and again. Yet he had survived against the odds. One thing he knew for certain was that he would be a victim no longer.

In the hours of wakefulness, the two meandered their way southwest toward the sea. Away from the wretched cavern and the broken tribes. Although the Nazca battle had ended the pursuit of Dwapek for a time, he knew that they would never stop searching for him, and to be captured would mean suffering the likes of which he could only imagine. Dwapek shook off the foreboding thoughts and swallowed hard, hoping the heaviness in his belly would subside. He looked over to the massive beast striding alongside him. The muscles under his brown and silver-streaked fur rolled with great strength and grace. Dwapek was feeling better with each rise, too. They stopped at a shallow stream to drink and Dwapek turned his gaze to the tangerine horizon glowing above gray, rocky outcroppings and his mind disappeared into the beauty and his hope. They were going to make it.

A frigid, slimy THWACK on Dwapek's cheek hurtled him from his reverie. "What in the Veld—?" A sizable trout flopped harmlessly on the icy grass at his feet and a drooling Maul dripped with water and comedy. "Maul! Not funny!" His scowl crumbled into laughter. Genuine laughter. When was the last time he had laughed like this?

He stooped and collected the fish in his arms. It wriggled and slapped while Maul crouched on all fours with his behind playfully wiggling high above his head. Dwapek started to heave the fish in Maul's direction but it slipped and Dwapek attempted to regain his grip.

Maul, anticipating the toss, had lunged forward, mouth agape while his glistening teeth snapped a breath from Dwapek's face, grazing the sleeves of his coat. At that moment, he was reminded that the bear was indeed still a savage creature capable of great destruction. Maul chewed a few times, unblinking, then sauntered back to the half-frozen creek where he had obtained the snack. Within minutes, Maul had swiped another smaller catch and nosed it toward Dwapek.

Dwapek shrugged, and tore into the raw fish. Once finished, the unlikely pair continued following the meandering stream west until a breeze swept in the scent of something new, something he'd been both anticipating, and dreading. The salty smell of the sea.

Dwapek swallowed hard; the sinewy meat stuck in his chest. He had known he would have to say good-bye, but hadn't expected it to be so difficult. He stopped and sat on a fallen tree, the trunk perfectly positioned for this purpose, and lowered his fish to his lap. He looked, really looked, at Maul. The bear too had stopped, and now sniffed the air, unaware of the gravity of what this change brought. He grunted then continued toward it.

Within a few hours, the smell of the sea grew unmistakable, having replaced completely the cold pine of the foothills through which they had been traveling. Dwapek crested a ridge and his breath caught. Before him, as far as the eye could see, was the deep blue of the sea.

Maul's ears perked up at the sound of a throaty roar reverberating through the sparse trees. Dwapek froze then braced himself, trying to keep completely silent, but readying his legs for action at a moment's notice. Time to run again. He slipped his hand into his pocket and rubbed his thumb across the blue stone, tightening his grip.

The sound repeated. Dwapek spotted Maul out of the corner of his eye, and realized his friend was not posturing defensively. Instead, he rose to a seated position, eyes piercing the foliage before suddenly bounding in the direction of the sound.

"Maul!" Dwapek anxiously yelled, a cold sweat on the back of his neck and a shake down his arms. Thankfully, Maul halted as quickly as he had begun, still staring off in the direction of the other creature. He released a sharp cry before turning back to Dwapek.

"What's out there, buddy?" Dwapek's voice quivered uncertainly as Maul lowered his blocky head to meet Dwapek's own, gentle puffs of breath warming his skin. Dwapek lifted his hands and began stroking the sides of Maul's face.

Maul whined and his large amber eyes shifted to the right, exposing bright white crescent moons before they met Dwapek's. And suddenly Dwapek knew that the time had come. Maul was ready to go.

Dwapek inhaled deeply and squeezed the giant bear's jowls, bringing their foreheads together. "Oh Maul . . ." was all that Dwapek could manage. He knew it was the right thing to do. He had been preparing for this. Now Maul, as if knowing Dwapek's innermost core, was setting the wheels into motion.

Dwapek cleared his throat. "You're right, of course. And better you have somewhere to go . . ." Dwapek paused and lifted his chin to the side and continued with an unexpected gruffness to his voice. "Let's get this collar off of you. Can't leave a mark for the Renziks to recognize you." *A bird cannot fly without wings and a path is only as good as its dirt.* Dwapek sent his mind into the iron collar searching for seams of weakness, and found two. The collar had been forged from two pieces of bent metal. Gripping these two seams with his mind, he drew upon the residual power stored within, as much as he could safely hold. Feeling such a volume of energy, Dwapek reached in and pulled out the blue stone. He had reason to believe his bones had fully recovered at this point, but wanted to keep it that way. *Better safe than suffering.*

Holding out his other hand, he sent the totality of this energy into the ground beside him, a spray of snow and sod littering the trees in that directing, leaving behind a sizable ditch.

Two half-circles of heavy iron fell from Maul's neck and hit the ground with a clang. Dwapek and Maul both stared at them dumbly. The broken collar screamed of their broken bond, of a friendship that could no longer be.

Dwapek had endured so many breakings in his short life. A broken Renzik code after calling to his mother, leaving behind a broken family. His relationship with his father had started as a crack that became a chasm, which effectively broke his engagement to Deleanor. Worst of all was the brokenness he felt inside in the midst of so much failure, so much upheaval.

The collar lay broken at his feet, and now it was over. A wash of emotions flooded Dwapek and shock turned to bitter frustration. He cried. Between sobs, his lips curled and he spat, "You're free. Get out of here. Go!"

But Maul did not leave. Instead, he poked at the collar with one paw, surprising Dwapek with his dexterity. Dwapek bent down, lifting the pieces. "These? What do you want?"

Maul sat on his haunches. And something unexpected happened. As Dwapek's thoughts swirled at the curious actions of the bear and the overwhelming sadness of losing a friend, an image appeared within the periphery of his thoughts. A river shimmered into existence with hundreds of fish leaping in the burbling current. On one side of the brook stood a silvertip bear, Maul, swatting at the myriad fish, tossing one every so often behind him. A shadow fell over the water, created by a vast bridge formed of land, which shot out from the middle of the river where Maul captured fish. On the far side of the bridge stood a small thick man in a long hide coat, smiling and laughing. The two exchanged a meaningful look from their respective positions, connected by this bridge, and their shared experience. Then, just like that, the vision was gone.

Dwapek blinked. Without further reflection, he picked up the two half-circles, matched them side by side, and placed them, ends down, onto the ground. He pressed and wiggled the arches into the hard dirt, leaving himself at one end and Maul diligently sitting on the other. Maul grinned. Well, rather, he opened his giant mouth into a pant and it seemed like he smiled.

Dwapek reached up and wrapped his arms around the front of Maul's neck, squeezing tight in an attempt to release the sadness he felt at saying good-bye. Just because it was the right course didn't mean it was a joyous one. His eyes watered, then flowed freely. And while Maul's did not likewise run wet, Dwapek knew he understood that they were separating, never to see each other again, and the sadness was palpable.

A roar sounded from behind, closer than before, though still concealed by the evergreen forest. Maul gave Dwapek one final appraising stare, then turned and raced in the direction of the sound. Dwapek tried to follow him through the trees, but the agile bear was too quick. He thought he caught a glimpse of another massive silver-and-brown-furred creature, but he couldn't be sure.

Dwapek gaped. Now Maul was gone, too.

He dragged his attention back to the iron harness-turned-bridge, and as he passed that place, he shuddered a sad sigh and continued straight ahead with warm rivulets streaking his cheeks, leaking into the corners of his mouth.

He inhaled, lifted his chin, and began his journey south along the coast. Perhaps Dwapek would not have had the fortitude to initiate their break. Maybe this was the Earthmother's subtle nod of grace. Perhaps Maul was not abandoning him; he was an animal, after all. An animal who did not know leave-taking etiquette, yet had the instinct to leave Dwapek with an image of hope. He had left Dwapek a bridge; and bridges only worked when two parts were torn asunder.

Dwapek had broken the laws of nature, broken the mores of the Renziks, and broken the boundaries between man and beast. But in so doing, he had been made whole. He flung his arms open wide to the sparse tufts of grass at his feet and a distant steel-gray sea of promise and possibility and ran toward the next breaking . . . and maybe, hopefully, a new bridge. Dwapek was broken, but he knew with near certainty that this was only temporary.

Thank you, Maul. May the Earthmother place her favor upon you and your kin.

As Dwapek started south along the sea's icy edge, the call of a different bear was returned by Maul's own joyous bawl, a reunion more unlikely than Dwapek's survival in the depths of the Nazca's lair. At least, Dwapek imagined it was so. He didn't dare turn back to see for himself, for he knew if he did, he might abandon this most difficult course indefinitely. To turn now would be the undoing of both bears as well as himself. He continued down, and repeated a new homage to the Earthmother. "Thank you. Thank you, Earthmother. Thank you for caring for your creations."

He didn't know what dangers his next life would bring, didn't even know for certain he would reach the land of men as intended. But it was the path set before him and he determined to endeavor. Clutching the blue stone that had both saved and cursed him, he continued one foot in front of the other toward the next chapter in his young life.

CHAPTER 16

Dwapek's sudden plunge into the world of men had been filled with trials, but paying for passage south had not been one.

"I don't see how that is possible," Dwapek had responded to the captain.

"It's quite simple." He spoke slowly so as to simplify the concept. "Someone gave me money to ensure you were well taken care of." He shrugged. "If you would like to give me more money, I will gladly accept."

Dwapek shook his head, a sinking feeling in his stomach. "Who? When?"

Captain Triggot scratched his long beard. "Well, let's see. Tall fellow, even by human standards. Approached a week or so before we were set to lift anchor. Handed me a purse of gold and said to be anchored here at Bodo for five days beginning in six turnings of the moons. Said there'd be a Renzik in need of travel south to the

Scritlandian city of Dysodos and if I provided him with such, there'd be twice this purse in it for me." He chuckled. "Figured the man was crazy, but I was already headed to these lands so it didn't make no difference to me. What sort of captain would I be to complain about accepting free money?"

This revelation sent chills up Dwapek's spine. How could anyone have anticipated his arrival on the ship months earlier? That was . . . well . . . impossible. "What did this man look like?"

This question seemed to vex Captain Triggot, who furrowed his brow in thought. "Strange, I . . . can't rightly recall. 'Twas dusk when we spoke." The captain closed his eyes as if visualizing the scene. "Yes, now I recall. The setting sun was behind him. Didn't really get a good look at his face. And . . . he wore a hood. Didn't much care once I smelled the gold."

Could this have been Targon? Was Targon even real?

No matter. While Dwapek did not care for the notion of being a part of someone else's machinations, Captain Triggot had been right. Dwapek was not in a position to disagree with free passage from a place filled with those who wished him harm.

"Whelp, I've a ship to run. You go on ahead and get settled in. I'll have Drat show you around." He pointed to a spindly, gray-bearded man currently pulling a rope to the right. "No such thing as idle passengers onboard the *Fero*." He turned and started toward the rear of the ship, then stopped and spun on his heel.

He held up his index finger. "Oh yes, I almost forgot. There's one other thing." He fumbled around in his pockets then held up a hand. "Stay right there. I know it's around here somewhere."

He disappeared into a cabin at the front of what looked to Dwapek like a monstrous floating wagon, then returned a few moments later holding something wrapped in a shiny silver cloth. "I'd have kept this for myself, but the man promised a healthy sum upon your delivery to the south." He placed the object into Dwapek's hands. "This is for you. The man said something to the effect of 'he's earned it.' I assume you know what he meant by that."

Dwapek unrolled the smooth, shiny fabric until the object inside became visible. An onyx blade shimmered in the winter sun. The Blade of Taldronis.

He laughed. A thunderous, throaty guffaw that drew uneasy stares from the human crew. Dwapek didn't care. The gods had won this bout. *Never again,* he thought as he handed the black blade back to the captain. *Every decision I make from now on is my own, beginning with this one.* "Take it. You've just as much right to it as I."

Captain Triggot eyed him skeptically before accepting the relic.

Dwapek walked to the side of the ship as the land of his birth slipped away. His hand reached down into the pocket of his coat to grip the blue stone. *Every single decision.*

Dwapek nodded absently as he continued to ponder the impossibilities of the last few weeks. Then his thoughts wandered toward the next chapter in his life. He concluded that he didn't much care where life took him so long as it didn't feature anything with more than four legs.

EPILOGUE

DWAPEK PICKED UP THE SCRITLANDIAN language quickly enough, beginning during the journey south. Whatever this new world threw his way, it would pale in comparison to what had driven him to depart the only home he'd ever known in the first place.

Five years later, initiate Dwapek of the Scritlandian order of monks had still not seen or heard from the man who called himself Targon. At least, not so far as he was aware. But he eventually made a few friends in the city.

Today he walked the busy streets of Scritler, a determined march in the stifling heat of the midday sun. His slight stature drew judgmental stares, but the brown robes of the faith prevented anyone from taking action.

Dwapek was on his way to see a specialist . . . of sorts. Not only was she famed for her travels, she was also said to be a master lapidary. In spite of this, she was not an easy woman to locate.

"Watch it!" yelled a man driving a cart on the wrong side of the street.

The color in his dark skin drained as he saw the robes. "I'm . . . my apologies. Tecuix bless you and your brethren."

Dwapek smiled. He received more respect here than he ever did among his own people. There were *some* benefits to having joined the order of monks. However, his reason for being on this side of town was not exactly sanctioned by the faith. That thought reminded him that he should probably not broadcast the fact that an initiate was visiting *her*. He withdrew his cloak from his pack and reluctantly pulled it over his robes. He was already sweating, but he did not wish for word of a halfling monk's travels to this part of town making its way back to the monastery.

The sun had moved about the width of hand by the time he arrived at the bakery that allegedly doubled as an entrance. A man pounded dough the way any baker might, and ignored Dwapek the way most humans did.

"Excuse me, sir."

The young muscular man stopped what he was doing and walked over to the counter directly in front of Dwapek. Ages of men were difficult to gauge because they lived only about half as long as Renziks, but he guessed the man hadn't seen many more than twenty summers. His sleeveless arms brimmed with sharp angular muscles, while his apron concealed a burgeoning belly. The young lad's business appeared to be going well enough that food was not a concern. Being paid extra as a bodyguard probably didn't hurt.

"What can I do for you?"

"I'm here to see the lapidary." Dwapek set two silver coins upon the counter, then stepped back to wait.

The man took the coins and investigated their authenticity, smelling, licking, and biting. Once satisfied, he opened a pantry cupboard that concealed a series of latches which opened up to a hallway behind.

Clever, thought Dwapek.

Gerold stepped through then called back, "Wait here." He reappeared soon after then gestured for Dwapek to enter. "Through here, knock seven times, then wait for the lapidary to greet you."

Dwapek did precisely as instructed. A few moments later, a middle-aged Scritlandian woman opened the door. She said nothing until she had crossed the room to return to her desk, which was cluttered with parchments, and the room was similarly filled with an array of books and scrolls, all alleged to have been acquired during her famed travels to every corner of the continent. Mixed in among the literature were several pieces of jewelry, all in various stages of assembly. Three oil lamps kept the windowless room well lit, shadows from various objects triangulating in the center of the room. The state of organized disarray gave the impression of a person with dozens of ongoing projects, each receiving attention in a system known only to the one in charge.

Her scowl seemed to eat away at what could have been an otherwise attractive woman. Her chocolate Scritlandian skin shone smooth like polished marble, yellow light in her large, knowing brown eyes. Branches of black hair adorned with red, blue, and green rubies spilled out from beneath a purple headdress and matching scarf.

"What brings you to my shop, brother . . ." She trailed off waiting for Dwapek to provide a name.

He instinctively pulled at his cloak to cover the brown robes of the order. *Too late, ice-brain.* "Dwapek. It's just Dwapek. I'm . . . I'm not ordained. Just an initiate."

She waved a hand as if swatting a cluster of flies. "Well, what brings you to my shop, *initiate* Dwapek?" Her tone suggested skepticism, which considering the way she attempted to keep her place of business hidden from the general passerby, should not have been unexpected. Considering the nature of her work—dealing in information, jewels, and artifacts of heretical nature—the presence of anyone associated with the Scritlandian order of monks would surely put her on the defensive. Not a good way to begin.

Dwapek reached into his pack and pulled out the blue stone sphere.

"I am hoping to have this stone cut into four pieces, each set into an amulet to be worn about the neck. An acquaintance of mine says you possess this skill."

"Hmm. Is that right? And who might this acquaintance of yours be?"

Dwapek looked up to find her eyes boring into his own. "His name is Draílock. He says you've done some work for him in the past."

The friendship Dwapek had formed with the elderly man was a story unto itself, but the man had proven resourceful and shared similar curiosities related to magic. He claimed to be a self-taught wizard of limited ability, but Dwapek sensed the man didn't reveal his skills to their fullest. Nevertheless, Dwapek had been grateful to make a friend in a place so unwelcoming to beings of Scritlandian folklore such as himself. Draílock being of a different ethnicity than the rest of the Scritlandian population gave them that immediate bond of a common struggle. Draílock had promised this woman was the best in the business, though a bit eccentric.

Dwapek wasn't certain, but he thought he caught a flutter in the woman's eyes at the mention of Draílock. She gave a warm smile, and the tone of her voice softened. "Yes, I have done some work for him in the past. You say he is a friend of yours?"

Dwapek nodded, sensing that Draílock had been underselling the nature of his relationship with the woman.

She rose from her chair and walked over to where Dwapek stood. "Well? Let's have a look-see." She extended her hand.

He hesitated. This stone meant so much to him. Handing it over to a complete stranger, friend of a friend or not, felt wrong. He swallowed a lump of reluctance, then placed it into her open palm.

She moved back toward her desk and bade him take a seat in front. She moved the stone from hand to hand, before lifting it to her eyes, inspecting it closely. "Hmm . . ." She shut one eye and squinted with the other. "Uh-huh . . ." Then Dwapek felt the slightest tingle of magic, followed by the familiar blue glow of the stone. Her stare returned to him and she grinned wide. "Ooh, I see. Quite unique. How much would you want for a piece of my own?"

"It's not for sale," he said, more firmly than intended.

She grinned. "Nothing is for sale until the right price is brought forth and then . . . ?" She flourished her hand to finish the thought.

"It is not for sale."

"My, my. Testy little Northman, aren't you? Very well. Not for sale. Well, my price then to work on such a stone is high, perhaps restrictively so. I don't believe that whoever made this item intended it to be cut."

Draílock didn't let on how much currency he had stowed away, but he had been confident in his ability to cover the cost. "Well? What's your price?"

She continued to eye the stone, though Dwapek was certain this was just for show. "Were you not a friend of Draílock"—she dragged out the sound of his name—"I would charge no less than twelve gold, but . . ."

Dwapek nearly choked on air. He needed to get this conversation back on topic. "I can't pay more than four golds, so if you're looking to rob me of more than that, I apologize for wasting your time."

She scowled. "Well, you're telling the truth about one thing. You really are a friend of Draílock. Trying to rob a poor, old spinster. I agree to this price. Six golds it is."

"I said I can't pay more than f—"

"Oh, please," she interrupted, annoyed. "You have five gold in your purse. You will pay the five now and return in one turn of the moon with the remaining piece, at which point I will hand over your completed amulets. Unless, of course, you'd like to reconsider sell—"

"Fine. Six golds," grumbled Dwapek, grinding his teeth. *I'm sending Draílock to collect. She'd fit right in with the roving tinkers back home. Except—no. That wasn't home. Not anymore.*

Worth the price, he told himself.

He rose to his feet, fished out the five gold coins, and set them roughly upon her desk before turning to leave.

"Initiate Dwapek."

He stopped and turned to face her, eyebrows up in question.

"A word of friendly advice." She paused until he nodded. "Next time you come looking to haggle with a witch, don't bring more than you're willing to spend." She winked as she scooped up the coins. "A pleasure doing business with you."

Dwapek didn't respond.

"And do give Draílock my best," she said in a throaty voice that confirmed the nature of their relationship.

"Good-bye, Ruka."

THANK YOU FOR READING

WORD-OF-MOUTH IS CRUCIAL FOR ANY author to succeed. If you enjoyed *To Wield a Plague*, please pay it forward by posting an honest review to Goodreads, Amazon, Bookbub, or wherever you post reviews.

Works by Derrick Smythe include:
Passage to Dawn series
Book 1 | The Other Magic
Book 2 | The Other Way
Book 3 | The Other Battle (TBD)
Book 4 | The Other Truth (TBD)

Passage to Dawn companions
Prequel 1 | To Earn the Sash
Prequel 2 | To Wield a Plague

READ ON FOR A SNEAK PEEK OF

THE OTHER MAGIC

YOUR SNEAK PEEK OF

THE OTHER MAGIC

Passage to Dawn: Book One

Aynward

[Excerpt]

Aynward followed the pageboy sent from the university, a lad of no more than ten summers. He wore a long purple robe with high slits on both sides, exposing his white hose. So far, every student he had spotted, few as that may be, had been wearing this exact same garb. But this boy couldn't possibly be a student, could he?

He had a few minutes before they arrived, so he decided to ask.

"You seem a bit young to be a student. Are you one of the counselor's servants or something?"

The boy stopped in his tracks and whipped around to face Aynward. "I'm no servant. I'm in *the program*." He turned and walked, faster now.

"Oh, right, *the program*. How could I have missed that?"

That comment met no response, and Aynward started to wonder if the remainder of the trek was doomed to silence. But the boy finally turned his head back slightly and said, "I work for the college to pay for secondary school. I learn what I'll need to know in order to get in once I know it."

"Hmm, I see. They're pretty strict on who they let past the gates; you just seem a bit young to be a student."

The youth didn't turn around. "They allow a number of us poppers to earn a place at the university. The count holds a competition each year, and the top three finishers earn a scholarship. I will still have to go through the testing just like everybody else, but I'll be ready in short order."

Aynward couldn't imagine a program like that going over well in Salmune. He could hardly believe that Brinkwell would allow urchins and peasants to learn alongside the nobles, but decided he didn't need to comment on that. He said, "Oh," and left it at that.

A few uneventful minutes later, they were passing beautiful buildings, shimmering in their gray-blue stone, ivy growing up the sides. The university was stirring, people passing from building to building in small numbers, all wearing the same purple robes accented by a chain necklace with a circular amulet marked by a

SNEAK PEEK: THE OTHER MAGIC

crest. He didn't get close enough to observe whether the crests were all the same.

The boy stopped at a door between several identical buildings.

"Open this door, take a right down the hallway, and knock on the third door on the left. Good day."

He scuttled away without another word.

Aynward stood there wondering what this meeting would bring. Nothing good, he presumed. But as his old friend Fronk would always say, "Nothing for it, but toward it." *Here we go.*

He followed the directions, found the door, and knocked. This was rewarded with the sound of rustling, then it opened. Aynward expected to meet the eyes of the person who had summoned him, but no one was there. He spotted a messy desk, scrolls strewn about, along with stacks of multi-size books, which lined the walls, as well. He had opened the door to the world's smallest, most compact library. Aynward's attention shot back to the door as it continued to move.

A child emerged from behind, turning away from him as he moved toward the messy desk. It wasn't until the child turned sideways that Aynward realized that this was no child after all. It was the tiniest man he'd ever seen!

The small person rounded the normal-size desk and ascended a little stool that led to the normal-size chair.

"You—you're not a child!" blurted Aynward. He was horrified the second the words left his mouth.

The little man didn't smile. "Well, you're a smart one, aren't you? What gave it away? Was it the beard? Must have been the beard."

"I'm sorry. I just—I've never seen a—I've never seen a person who looked like you."

The man couldn't have been more than half his own height. He had matted, ear-length hair, cropped by a long red beard. He wore a purple robe trimmed in yellow and two thickly chained amulets, one resembling those worn by the other students, the other housing a large blue gemstone.

"Never seen a Renzik in person, I take it. Aye, we don't make our way down to the lands of the big'ns all too often. We're a bit of a cliquey folk, to be sure. I'll try not to be offended by your ignorance."

Aynward had heard stories of the northern folk, mostly fables and nightmare-type stories told to children before bedtime. Most believed they weren't real; Aynward was no longer among them.

"You're likely wondering why you're here or assuming incorrectly why you're here, so let me clear that up before we go any further."

It struck Aynward then: the man's voice. He'd heard it yesterday during the testing. It was unmistakable, the halting sound to his speech, the odd way of cutting off sounds at the end of his words before they were finished, like he was in a hurry to spit each word out before he changed his mind. This man had insulted him. He played it back in his mind—*arrogant, privileged, and entitled*, to be specific. These insults had, however, motivated him to go back and figure out the riddle of the last scroll, but the audacity was still infuriating. He'd had no right. Aynward's face warmed as he remembered the insults.

His anger was interrupted by the half-man. "I am Counselor Dwapek. And you're here because I have convinced the testing council to allow me to take you on as my pupil."

"Pupil?" responded Aynward dumbly, still reeling from his recognition of the voice.

"Yes, you will be my pupil, I your adviser," responded Dwapek.

Aynward was thoroughly confounded. This man, or half-man, or Renzik, or whatever he was, had insulted him more harshly than anyone in his entire life, save Dolme himself, but then turned around and volunteered to take him on as his pupil? Perhaps pupil is something different here in the Isles.

"So what does this mean, exactly?"

The man folded his miniature hands in front of him and rested them on the desk.

"It means I was told by the simpletons on the council that it is part of my duty to work with and advise at least one pupil. With much reluctance, I have selected you. You've been enrolled in the courses I saw fit and I shall ensure that you satisfy all academic requirements while under my tutelage."

"But why? It was you yesterday who berated me at the end of the testing, was it not? Why choose me after all that?"

He chuckled. "Oh, that? I suppose my northern accent gave it away. Can't seem to shed it. Guess I'm just not made for subtlety."

Aynward bristled, but Dwapek didn't give time to interrupt. "In spite of what I said yesterday, I did see a sliver of potential beneath that thick layer of egotism you wear like second skin. You're smart. Though that doesn't take much. Being smart is merely the act of appearing less stupid than everyone else around you, which, considering the other enrollees—still." He paused and smiled wide. "The way the other counselors drooled over your quick work of the test, I couldn't help but stake my claim, in my fashion. And none of the other big'ns wanted you after what I'd said. They're all too fickle and driven by impulse and emotion. I changed the entire room's mind about you in seconds. I don't care for wasting time arguing over pupils when there's so much else that needs doing."

He held up his finger for effect. "But to be clear, this doesn't mean I truly think you hold much promise. I'm quite confident in my initial assessment of you."

Aynward opened his mouth to set the man straight but was interrupted.

"Yes, yes, you have a million and two insults for me. I'm going to firmly decline to be an audience for that. As I said, I've more important business. Such as getting you set for tonight's festivities. Classes start tomorrow, and you can't be walking around the university looking like some foreign noble idiot. Better get you the robes and crest. This'll get you into the exclusive university pub down the street, as well." He winked and pulled out a small scroll.

How did he—

"Your father, and by proxy, the dean, has made it very clear that you're to study jurisprudence, the science of the elite, as they say. You're quite capable of doing so. I see no need for academic remediation: yesterday's testing revealed full mastery of the trivium's grammar, rhetoric, and logic. You'll start immediately with the following courses: Foundations of Thomist Law, Althusian Ethics, and Apotheca."

Aynward was confused by the last one. "Apotheca? Why would I be taking a course in potion making? What does that have to do with law?"

Dwapek smiled, and the blue gemstone that hung around his neck caught a glimmer of light, appearing to almost glow with excitement. "Why, nothing at all. But trees don't always grow in the forest." Aynward waited for further explanation, but the little man seemed content with the vague non-answer. He continued, "You'll also be taking—"

Aynward cut him short, frustrated that his question had been ignored. "None of what you said makes any sense. If this course has nothing to do with law, why am I taking it?"

Dwapek's expression switched back and forth between smug satisfaction and annoyance. Aynward wasn't sure the man had the ability to express any other mood. His face settled on smug; Aynward decided that he hated him already.

"Apothecarian knowledge will not help you rule or advise others, but it may one day keep you alive when cowardly enemies attempt to kill you or those in your care. Therefore, it is standard university practice to require those students we think capable to take this course. It seems that when people are alive, they do more things worth being proud of. It's good advertisement for us when our graduates go on to live long enough to utilize the knowledge and skills they acquire while here. After all, the wind swirls something nasty to the west."

Aynward rolled his eyes at the furtive insult wrapped with another nonsensical proverb.

"Point taken," he said in defeat. Is apothecarian even a real word?

"Good, good! You're getting the picture." He pointed somewhere to Aynward's right and said, "Now be a good little big'n and get yourself some proper garb. The council simply won't abide our students walking around looking like regular folk, or, in your case, spoiled foreign gentry." He chuckled to himself, or maybe for Aynward's benefit, he couldn't be sure. "Don't get blue on me, laddie. I'm merely cleansing you of your former

SNEAK PEEK: THE OTHER MAGIC

lack of humility. I'll ease up once you've accepted an appropriate reduction in self-worth."

Aynward was furious, confused, and speechless. He stood there dumbly, trying to process everything the man had said, along with what the man had actually meant, or what Aynward thought he might have intended to mean.

"Run along. I've work to do. Get yourself dressed and fed before tonight's festivities. The desposition is mandatory before enrollment becomes official."

"So I've heard," he said, thinking back to the university pub.

"Good. Two doors down on the right. Tell the man that Dwapek sent you. See you tonight."

Aynward finally found his tongue again. "Where do I go for this desposition?"

"University square. That's right; need your schedule, too. Classes begin tomorrow. Here, here. You take this. I've got it written here." He pointed to his temple.

He rolled the tiny parchment back up and tossed it Aynward's way.

Aynward caught the mini scroll in his left hand and vacated the room as quickly as possible. Never before had he been forced to backpedal his emotions like this. The smaller-than-life man had put him on the defensive the moment he'd entered, and he still wasn't sure where he'd landed by the end. It was like being in a room with his father, but without the throne and all the yelling. He was pretty certain he hated the little man, but couldn't put his finger on why. Was it the way Dwapek pattered him with insults like a steady rain? That was likely part of it. Then why was he struggling to identify how he felt about the whole exchange? It should have been cut and dry.

Then it dawned on him. He hated Dwapek, but there was more to it than that. He also felt some measure of respect for the little man who was willing to insult someone whose kingdom would likely not even give him an audience because of his stature alone, not to mention that he was likely of ignoble birth. Yet the man treated him much the same as Dolme did, but without all the self-righteousness. Aynward hated Dwapek to be sure, but he also felt a desire to prove the man's assessment of him wrong, something he couldn't say about his relationship with Dolme.

All this took place in the time it took him to pick up his student uniform, all three sets, as well as a thick-chained amulet with the university crest. He donned the first robe and tights, placed the amulet around his neck, then headed back to his aunt's house. He dropped off the extra sets of uniforms then went in search of a good meal. Dolme insisted on escorting him while the city was still new to him.

He frowned when Aynward showed him the parchment with his schedule but said nothing more than, "Good. You're enrolled now."

They ate in silence, which Aynward appreciated. He had a lot to think about.

SNEAK PEEK: THE OTHER MAGIC

Hours later, he ventured back to the university for the mandatory induction ceremony. He was wearing his purple robes, which were surprisingly light, as well as the crested amulet around his neck; an image of a scroll with a sword protruding from its spine to symbolize the power of knowledge, the hallmark of the university.

He was holding it in his hand as he passed the gates and crossed the campus to the university square. He stopped in his tracks when he saw the crowd of hooded figures that formed a circle in the middle. It must have been the entire student population. A few of the nearest hoods turned to face him. Their faces were obscured by shadow, but he could feel their sinister smiles.

Three moved toward him. He stood motionless as they approached. As they guided him toward the center, his heart began pounding. The men at the center were wearing the robes lined by yellow, the counselors. They were wearing masks.

About the Author

DERRICK SMYTHE HAS BEEN FASCINATED with all things elvish, dwarvish, and magical since his days of running through the woods with sharpened sticks in defense of whatever fortification he and his brothers had built that summer. After consuming nearly every fantasy book he could find, he was driven to begin work on one of his own. When he isn't dreaming up new stories, he can be spotted hiking the Adirondack Mountains or traveling the world. He currently resides near his hometown in upstate New York with his enchanting wife, ethereal daughters, and his faithful-if-neurotic Australian Shepherd, Magnus.

Derricks Smythe's debut novel, *The Other Magic*, is the award-winning first installment of his passage to dawn series, an epic fantasy set in the World of Doréa.

To learn more about Derrick and his work visit:
Website: derricksmythe.com
Facebook: derricksmythe.author
Email: author@derricksmythe.com

Printed in Great Britain
by Amazon